ITALY WITH
THE BILLIONAIRE BOYS CLUB

CARA MILLER

Want my unreleased 5000-word story
Introducing the Billionaire Boys Club
and other free gifts from time to time?

Then join my mailing list at

http://www.caramillerbooks.com/inner-circle/

Subscribe now and read it now!

You can also follow me on Twitter and Facebook

An Invitation from the Billionaire Boys Club

———

Midnight with the Billionaire Boys Club

———

Dreaming with the Billionaire Boys Club

———

A Promise from the Billionaire Boys Club

———

Engaged to the Billionaire Boys Club

———

A Surprise from the Billionaire Boys Club

———

Romance with the Billionaire Boys Club

———

A Billionaire Boys Club Wedding

———

Honeymoon with the Billionaire Boys Club

———

Billionaire Boys Club Babies

———

Italy with the Billionaire Boys Club

———

Life with the Billionaire Boys Club

Kelsey stood silently, completely surprised by Devin's words.

Everyone was so still, Kelsey thought she could hear her heart beat.

"That's not true," she said, in almost a whisper. She was willing herself not to cry.

"Devin. My office, now," Bill Simon said sharply. "The rest of you, start packing up."

Bill turned and began striding back to his side of the office, Devin gave a quick, defiant look to Kelsey, then followed behind Bill.

Kelsey took one look at the shocked expressions on the rest of her co-workers' faces.

"Excuse me," she said. Then she left.

She managed to close her office door before her tears began to fall. Kelsey angrily wiped them from her face with the back of her hand.

She had worked so hard to be taken seriously as a professional, and with one accusation, her hard work was wiped away.

Kelsey stood, her back against the door for another moment, trying to regain her focus and continuing to wipe tears from her eyes. Questions rose into her head, looking for an answer.

Kelsey knew that Devin didn't have any particular issue with her. It was simply that Bill respected her in a way that he didn't respect Devin, and Devin was jealous because of it. In her heart, Kelsey knew it wasn't personal, although at this moment, it felt more personal than anything.

However, there was one question that Kelsey didn't have the answer for, but knew that she needed to find out, if she had any hope of having a career in the close-knit Seattle legal community.

Where had Devin heard the rumor about Kelsey and Alex?

Kelsey had dried most of her tears — although she knew her eyes were still red — when there was a knock on the door.

"Come in," Kelsey said. Red eyes were nothing compared to the humiliation that she had just experienced.

Millie looked in, several flat boxes in her hand.

"You OK?" Millie asked in concern.

Kelsey nodded. "I'm all right," she replied. Millie walked into the office and set the boxes on the floor next to the client table. She closed the door behind herself.

"Marie told everyone the truth, that you left Collins Nicol because of Tyler's mom," Millie said.

Kelsey felt a weight lift from her shoulders. But she knew that Devin couldn't possibly be the only one who had heard the rumor. She needed to get to the bottom of who was passing it around.

Millie looked around Kelsey's office. "Do you need help?"

"It's fine," Kelsey said. "I don't have a lot to move."

"Let me know," Millie said.

"Thanks, Millie," Kelsey said. Millie gave her a gentle smile and left the office, closing the door behind herself.

Kelsey walked over and picked up one of the boxes. As she began to assemble it on her desk, there was another knock on her door.

"Come in," Kelsey said. The door opened, and Kelsey felt a jolt as she looked at her visitor.

Devin looked at her, but without the defiant look that he had had on his face fifteen minutes earlier. In fact, he seemed to want to avoid Kelsey's eyes.

"I'm sorry," he said, hesitantly, as if he was surprised to be saying it.

"OK," Kelsey said, although it wasn't.

"I didn't know… never mind," Devin continued, interrupting himself. "I was wrong, and I shouldn't have attacked you."

Kelsey looked at him. She wasn't sure what to say.

"Sorry, Kelsey," Devin said. He abruptly turned to leave.

"Devin?" Kelsey said. Devin turned back.

"Who told you that lie? About me and Alex?" she asked. She had no desire to know, but she needed to.

Devin was quiet for a moment, as if debating whether to tell her.

"Jamie Harding," he said quickly, then he left.

Kelsey let out a giant sigh and leaned against her desk. She felt both relief and distress. Relief, because Jamie worked at Collins Nicol, so perhaps the rumor hadn't gone too far. Distress, because that meant that there was someone in Collins Nicol who still held a grudge against Kelsey. And Kelsey didn't need to think too hard about who that person was. She knew it wasn't Jamie Harding — he barely knew Kelsey. Jamie was merely the messenger.

It was Mary White.

It all made perfect sense to Kelsey. She had turned down Mary's offer to return to Collins Nicol — and by doing so had put Mary in a bad spot with the firm. So why not spread a rumor that the firing had been justified? And in the process make Alex, a rising star at Collins, who was also a rival for Mary's position at the firm, look bad too?

Kelsey had to begrudgingly admit it was genius. But now, what — if anything — could she do?

She was still thinking about the question when Jake walked into her open door a while later. His suit jacket was off, and his white shirt sleeves were rolled up.

"Can I move your boxes for you?" he asked.

"It's fine. I only have three," Kelsey replied.

"The books are probably heavy," Jake said, lifting the box closest to himself.

Kelsey looked at him curiously. "Is Devin's office clear?" she asked.

"It's clear of him," Jake said.

"What do you mean?" Kelsey asked.

"Devin is on unpaid leave until at least the end of the month," Jake said as he and Kelsey walked out of her office.

"Really?"

"Bill told him not to come back unless he had a note stating that he had volunteered for 50 hours at the Women's Law Center. Plus, Devin had to apologize to each one of us individually about his behavior. Bill's furious."

Jake glanced at Kelsey.

"You know none of us believed Devin, right?" he asked her.

Kelsey hadn't actually given it any thought. She had been too stunned by the accusation.

"He's such a jerk," Jake went on, "He's lucky Bill didn't fire him. I don't know what Devin was thinking, Bill not going to give you an office because of a rumor?" They reached Kelsey's new office and Jake set the box down on the desk. The office was clear. Six boxes sat next to the door.

"It doesn't matter," Kelsey said.

"Well, at least it doesn't for the week. I wonder if Devin's going to come back," Jake said. "I can't imagine him volunteering for anything that didn't help himself."

"Devin's going to need Bill's recommendation to go to another firm," Kelsey said. "I don't think he's going to want to leave on a bad note."

"True," Jake said. He looked around the office. "Not much of a view, but there's a lot more space," he commented.

"It's quieter," Kelsey noted. In her current office, every so often the sounds of the reception desk traveled to her desk.

"I'll get the rest," Jake said. He glanced at Devin's boxes. "And I'll get these out of here," he added.

"Thanks, Jake," Kelsey said. Jake gave her a smile, and left.

"What are you thinking about, Princess?" Tyler asked that evening. Kelsey was lying in his arms, looking up at the ceiling. The lights had been off for a while, but Kelsey hadn't yet managed to fall asleep.

"Work," Kelsey admitted. "You?" she asked. Tyler obviously hadn't been able to sleep either.

"Me too," he said.

"You don't usually bring your work home," Kelsey said, hoping that he would discuss his work instead of her own. She hadn't told Tyler about Devin's accusation, and didn't particularly want to discuss it with him. Alex Carsten was a sore spot with Tyler.

"It's been a long week," Tyler said, cuddling against her. She felt his warm skin against her shoulder, and she smiled happily.

"Do you want to talk about it?" Kelsey asked.

"Not really," Tyler said. "You?"

"Nope," Kelsey agreed.

"OK," Tyler said, giving her a kiss. "Do you want to sleep?"

"Not yet," Kelsey said. "We could talk about something other than work."

"Italy?" Tyler asked. "We leave in two weeks."

"I know, I can't wait," Kelsey said. After having spent an entire weekend with Tyler last week, the thought of spending three weeks alone with him was irresistible.

"Have you thought of anything you want to see while we're there?" Tyler asked.

"No," Kelsey said.

"Nothing at all?"

"I haven't had time to think about it," Kelsey said. "Have you?"

"I told Jeffrey to make us a list," Tyler said.

Kelsey giggled. "Did you really?" she asked.

"I haven't had time during the day lately to think," Tyler said.

"Are you sure you don't want to talk about work?" Kelsey pressed.

Tyler was silent for a moment. He stroked Kelsey's hair.

"I just don't know how I'm going to get past the proxy fight," Tyler said.

"I'm sorry," Kelsey said.

"Why are you sorry?" Tyler asked curiously.

"Because I know I'm part of the reason for the proxy fight," Kelsey replied.

"Kelsey, this doesn't have anything to do with you," Tyler said firmly. "I would have brought the proxy fight eventually anyway. I've hated Lisa's board for a long time. I just underestimated how much everyone at the company was going to react to my actions. Now I've got to pay the price."

"What's going on?" Kelsey asked.

"It's a lot of little things," Tyler said. "I'm not invited to meetings I need to be in, I'm shut out of events I need to go to. It's just very frustrating. Like Becks said, no one trusts that I have the best interests of the company in mind."

"Lisa does."

"Yes, she does. So does Bob. Just about everyone else, though, they think I'm just there for the money."

"Why else would you be there? It's a job, right?" Kelsey asked.

"Tactec sees itself as a family. And everyone thinks that I don't have family values. There's actually a rumor that I'm going to split the company up and sell it if I become CEO."

A rumor, Kelsey thought bitterly, but she said nothing.

"I don't know. I think Becks is going to try to solve this by throwing you, me, and Lisa in front of the cameras. Make us look like we're doing whatever normal families do."

Kelsey giggled again. "What do normal families do?" she asked.

"I don't have a clue. Lisa doesn't either. My childhood was spent drawing on the blank pages of annual reports and sitting in Lisa's office doing my homework while she negotiated with suppliers and argued with engineers. I'm not sure what the employees think I'm missing, but I guess Becks will figure it out."

"I'll help however I can," Kelsey said.

"Thanks," Tyler said, hugging her. "But remember, you have a life. I don't want you to get stressed out again because you're being Mrs. Olsen."

"I know. I won't," Kelsey said.

"OK," Tyler said. "What time can you leave work tomorrow?"

"Maybe three? I have some things I need to finish up before we leave."

"I'll pick you up then," Tyler said. Kelsey turned in his arms and stroked his face with her hand. Tyler kissed her in the dark.

"I am the luckiest man in the world," he said, and Kelsey closed her eyes, smiling as Tyler held her.

"One more week," Jessica said the next afternoon. Rory was nestled in Jess's lap, fast asleep, as Kelsey sat with a yawning Allie in her own lap. Allie was wrapped in an impossibly-soft cashmere baby blanket. Kelsey reached out and tucked the blanket around Allie's tiny pajama-covered foot, which had slipped out.

"It's terrible," Jess continued. "I love having Mom here, but I hate not being able to leave, so she needs to go."

Kelsey laughed at Jess's words.

"I'm just sayin'," Jess said, which made Kelsey laugh harder. The phrase was a favorite of Morgan's, who was on Kelsey's mind. Morgan's birthday was coming up, and Kelsey was in the process of deciding what to send to her.

As Morgan's on-again-off-again relationship with Bob Perkins was currently off, this year Morgan would not be going to Spain for her birthday. Although Morgan would never talk about it, Kelsey knew that she was still upset about the fact that Bob wouldn't marry her. Kelsey wanted to get something special for Morgan, so that Morgan would know that she was loved by her friends at the very least.

"I'm just worried about what Daddy's reaction is going to be," Jessica said.

"Your mom isn't concerned, right?" Kelsey asked.

"No. But I think she's deluding herself," Jessica replied.

"Really, Jess? She's been married to him for over 30 years."

"And for 30 years, she's been doing exactly what she's supposed to do. You saw what happened when I disobeyed him," Jessica said, and Kelsey involuntarily shivered. She had seen Dr. Hunter's reaction, and even now — over a year later — Kelsey still couldn't quite believe it.

"Has she talked to him since she left?" Kelsey asked.

"I don't think so," Jessica said. "Mom said that it's going to be fine, and there's nothing I can do anyway. She's got patients to see on Tuesday, so she's leaving no matter what."

"If she's not worried, I'm sure she'll be fine," Kelsey said hopefully. She knew that Jess was anxious, and since there was nothing that could be done about the situation, all Kelsey could do was be supportive.

"I hope so," Jessica said. She looked up as Ryan and Tyler walked into the room, each carrying a large tray.

"Aw, they're both sleeping," Ryan said, setting his tray on the enormous coffee table in front of the girls.

"Like they do anything else," Jessica teased, but she said it with a smile at the sleeping Rory.

"Aren't you supposed to enjoy it?" Tyler asked, setting his tray down next to Ryan's.

"Yeah, remember what Lisa said," Ryan said. "Here, let me take her," he said to Kelsey, removing the now sleeping Allie from her arms.

"What did Lisa say?" Tyler asked.

"Because you know it was about you," Jessica teased.

"Lisa said that you hated sleeping, even as a newborn. She never understood why people said that babies sleep all of the time, because you never did," Ryan said, as he removed Rory from Jessica's arms and put him gently in the bassinet next to his sister.

"My favorite story," Jess said, as she took a cut sandwich from the tray that Tyler had brought in, "was about how Lisa fell asleep standing up because she was so tired."

Tyler laughed. "Really?" he asked.

"She was walking into the kitchen to get a bottle of milk for you, and a few minutes later, she woke up, leaning against a wall. She said that was the moment she decided that she needed to work on weekends. At least at her firm, she could get some sleep by hiding under her desk," Jessica said.

"That's so sad," Tyler said as he laughed.

"Bro, you were really mean to her."

"It wasn't on purpose," Tyler replied. "I was a baby."

"A mean baby," Jessica giggled.

"It's turned out OK for her," Tyler said. "If she hadn't been worried about being able to feed me, she wouldn't have come up with the idea for Tactec."

"Is that true?" Kelsey asked, taking a drink from the tray.

"That what she said. Her law firm put her on the mommy track the second she got pregnant, so she knew she wasn't going to make partner. And Chris couldn't support us. It was up to Lisa to pay the rent."

"Wow," Kelsey said.

"Why did Bob decide to join Lisa and create Tactec?" Jessica asked. "He didn't need the money."

Kelsey knew that Bob had been a very successful white-collar-crime defense attorney before meeting Lisa Olsen, but like Jess, she didn't know exactly why he had left.

"Bob wanted to make a lot more money," Ryan said, taking a sandwich of his own. "He knew he couldn't make it billing himself out by the hour. Tactec makes money 24 hours a day."

This concept wasn't new to Kelsey. As a lawyer, she was limited by the number of hours she could work in a day. Of course a lawyer could become a billionaire, but it wasn't likely to happen through billing clients at an hourly rate.

"That worked out well for Bob then," Jessica said, taking her sandwich apart. "What's in this?"

Ryan smiled at her with his bright blue eyes.

"Something healthy," he replied.

Jessica closed the sandwich and took a bite. After she had chewed she said, "I knew it. When do I get to eat what I want?"

"Never. You're a mother now. You have a responsibility to stay healthy for your children," Ryan replied.

Kelsey ate a bite of her own sandwich. It tasted like chicken salad, but very slightly different.

"It's tofu," Jessica confirmed when Kelsey glanced at her. "Ryan's thinking about going vegetarian."

"We'll see. I don't eat a lot of meat anyway," Ryan said.

"Bob won't approve," Tyler commented.

"He's not here to object," Jess replied. "He's in the south of France."

"That's this year's vacation?" Kelsey asked.

Ryan glanced at her. "Yeah, not Spain," he replied, with a knowing look.

"Yes, Ryan, we all know that Bob isn't going out with Morgan," Tyler said in irritation. "Leave Kelsey out of it."

"I was just saying where Bob was," Ryan shrugged.

"How long will he be there?" Kelsey asked, addressing her question to Jessica.

"Two weeks. He gets back just after you guys leave," Jessica said, pulling a sliced red grape from the tofu salad in her sandwich and eating it.

"Looking forward to your trip?" Ryan asked.

Tyler glanced at Kelsey, and she felt herself blush.

"Very much," Tyler replied.

"Does my bride want waffles for breakfast?" Tyler asked Kelsey on Sunday morning.

Kelsey reached out and pulled Tyler towards herself.

"First," she said, "I want you."

"These are really great, Tyler." Kelsey said hours later, as she sat on the sofa with Tyler. She dipped her warm waffle into the Norwegian chocolate-hazelnut spread that Tyler had put out on the coffee table.

"I'm glad you like them," Tyler replied.

Kelsey's silk robe fell down her shoulder as she reached for her coffee. Tyler reached his hand out, and gently lifted it back up.

"Thanks," Kelsey said.

"Anytime, Princess," Tyler replied.

"I'm sorry I have to work," Kelsey said to him.

"You work for Bill Simon. I understand," Tyler replied. Because Kelsey was taking three weeks off, and because the two IP summer associates were about to leave, Kelsey needed to catch up on a few things that had been sitting on her desk for a while. "I'm glad you can work here, though."

"Work. Not play," Kelsey warned.

"It's not my fault that you're getting a late start," Tyler pointed out.

"Of course it is. You're irresistible," Kelsey replied.

Tyler leaned over and nuzzled her neck. "Are you sure we can't have more play time?" he whispered.

Kelsey glared at him. "Positive," she said, biting her waffle.

"I bet I can change your mind," Tyler said, sliding his hand up her thigh.

Kelsey hit his hand with the waffle. "I bet you can too. No," she said. Tyler grinned at her, and wiped off the chocolate-hazelnut spread that Kelsey had smeared on his hand. "Tyler, I don't want to have to take work to Italy," she said.

"I don't want you to either," Tyler conceded. "We'll save play time for later."

"Thank you," Kelsey said.

"What are you working on?" Tyler asked.

"Everything," Kelsey replied.

"Are you sure that you won't have to take work on our honeymoon?" Tyler asked doubtfully.

"Bill knows if I do, then you'll intervene with Lisa. So, no, it's fine," Kelsey said.

"Good. Mr. Simon's learned something," Tyler replied.

"About what?"

"About getting in my way," Tyler replied.

Kelsey giggled.

"What's so funny?"

"You need to learn to get along with people," Kelsey teased.

"I get along fine with you," Tyler replied.

Kelsey offered Tyler her waffle, and he took a bite.

"You certainly do," Kelsey admitted.

"Becks and I are having lunch tomorrow. Do you want to come?" Tyler asked later in the evening.

"Do you need me to?" Kelsey asked. "I was going to go shopping for our trip."

"You don't have to come to lunch," Tyler said. "But you know that you can just send Jeffrey to buy things for you."

Kelsey blushed. She was planning on buying lingerie.

"I think I'd rather buy these things myself," she replied.

Tyler gave her a smile.

"I see. Then it's fine. I'll deal with Becks myself. She's probably going to be shouting at me anyway." Tyler looked at Kelsey for a moment, then added, "Don't forget to take your new cards when you go shopping."

Kelsey bit her lip. The envelope that Tyler's financial advisors had given her was still in the bottom of her tote bag, unopened.

Tyler surveyed her.

"You haven't spent a dime of our money," he commented.

"It's not ours, it's yours," Kelsey said.

Tyler frowned. "What did I tell you?" he said.

"I just haven't gotten around to it."

"What is there to do? Take a card and pay for something. You've had access to those accounts for over two weeks, and you haven't bought as much as a Starbucks from them."

"Fine," Kelsey said in defeat. "Do I have a limit?" she asked, just a little sassily.

Tyler looked at her seriously. "You have to spend ten thousand dollars a month," he said firmly.

Kelsey frowned. "Tyler," she protested.

"Twenty thousand? More?" Tyler teased.

"Tyler," Kelsey repeated. "There's no way I can spend that kind of money."

"Of course you could. Jess does."

"Jess goes shopping all the time, and buys things for everyone, including me."

Tyler shrugged. "Buy something for Jess," he said.

"Jess doesn't need anything and she buys everything she wants."

"Start spending money, Kelsey."

Kelsey crossed her arms.

"You don't spend a lot of money," she said.

"Kelsey," Tyler said patiently. "We've discussed this a million times. You said that you would stop spending your own money once we got married. We've been married for seven weeks, and nothing. You promised."

Kelsey opened her mouth to say something, but then closed it. Tyler was right. She stood up from the sofa.

"Hang on," she said. Kelsey walked into the bedroom and picked up the tote that was sitting there. She returned to Tyler with the tote in her hands, and sat next to him, putting it on the coffee table.

Tyler watched her as Kelsey extracted her slate-blue Hermes wallet and the envelope holding the debit and credit cards from the advisors. Kelsey opened her wallet and removed her own debit and credit card. She handed them to Tyler.

"Here," she said as he took them.

Tyler smiled at her. "I'll put them in your desk drawer," he said.

"OK," Kelsey said. She picked up the envelope, and felt the smooth, expensive paper under her fingers. Then she opened it.

Inside there were three cards and a note. The note simply listed the PIN numbers of each card. Kelsey knew she would need to memorize them. She glanced at the cards. Two were debit cards from local banks. The third was a black credit card. Kelsey looked at it curiously, because a while back she had read about this particular card in a business magazine.

"There's no limit on the black one," Tyler said, confirming Kelsey's thoughts.

"No limit?" Kelsey said in disbelief.

"None," Tyler replied.

"So I could buy a car with this card?"

"They would probably check to make sure that it's you, but yes, you could. Do you want a new car?"

"No," Kelsey said, glancing at Tyler, who gave her a smile.

Kelsey sighed. She wanted to protest, but there was no point. Tyler had always been generous to Kelsey, and she knew from long experience that her complaints about his generosity were always ignored.

"How much are in the debit card accounts?" Kelsey asked.

"Go to the ATM and find out."

"I think not," Kelsey said. "Enough for a Starbucks?"

"I'm pretty sure," Tyler replied.

"Enough to buy Starbucks every day for the rest of my life?" Kelsey asked.

"Could be," Tyler said with a smile.

Kelsey sighed again. "Thank you," she said.

"You're welcome," Tyler replied.

"So you get a report of how much money I spend?"

"I get a message once a week and a full report every month," Tyler replied. "It's not just how much you spend, it's how much we spend."

"Let me guess, your section reads 'five trips to Starbucks, total cost, thirty dollars.'"

"Remember Kelsey, I have Jeffrey to spend my money for me. I don't need to spend any on my own."

"I guess," Kelsey conceded. "Do you really expect me to spend ten thousand dollars a month?"

"No, but I do want you to spend our money when you want something.

25

Invest your salary," Tyler's chocolate-brown eyes smiled at her. "Save for your own business."

"Maybe," Kelsey said, and she smiled just a little at the reminder. Ages ago, she and Tyler had discussed the possibility of Kelsey one day starting her own company, much like Lisa Olsen, and at the time, Kelsey had discussed how she wanted to have earned the money herself. Now that her student loans were almost completely paid off, it was certainly something that she could save for.

"So what will you buy first?" Tyler asked.

"Something for you," Kelsey replied.

"Really? What?"

"You'll see it in Rome," Kelsey said. "In bed," she added.

Tyler gave her a sexy grin.

"I'll look forward to it," he replied.

Kelsey walked down Fifth Avenue in a navy-blue sheath dress and Chanel flats, both gifts from Jessica. She had decided to take a long lunch now, just in case things got busier. She and Tyler would leave for Italy a week from Friday, on their second month anniversary.

As Kelsey walked into the lingerie shop where she had bought many of the things that she had worn on their first honeymoon, she smiled to herself. So much had happened over the weeks they had been together, but one thing hadn't changed at all.

She was still totally, blissfully, in love.

Tyler as Kelsey's husband was virtually the same as he had been as a boyfriend. Thoughtful, kind, and loving. On the flip side, he continued to push Kelsey out of her comfort zone, and despite her irritation, she knew that she needed it. Tyler believed that he had become a better person thanks to Kelsey, and she believed that it was true for her as well.

Tyler Olsen saw the Kelsey that she wanted to be.

Because she struggled to see the Kelsey that Tyler was in love with, Kelsey knew that she needed to grow more. Today, using Tyler's money, was one of those steps toward growth.

Kelsey looked around the store for a moment, then sighed in dismay. She had been recognized. Two saleswomen were whispering to each other near the counter. It wasn't surprising. The magazine that had featured Kelsey and Tyler's wedding had sold out across not only the Seattle area, but also across the country. The publisher had needed to go back to press for an additional run of copies. Kelsey had been surprised, and a little bit upset, but it was just another reminder that she had married a billionaire.

Kelsey turned before she could be spoken to, and walked out of the store. She stood on the street in the hot August sun for a moment. Normally, she wouldn't have cared so much about being recognized, but lingerie was kind of personal. It was why she hadn't sent Jeffrey out to buy it for her. And the last thing Kelsey wanted was an Instagram post by a rogue employee about what the new Mrs. Tyler Olsen had bought at a lingerie store.

She briefly considered returning to the office and ending her shopping trip, but she decided to walk over to the mall instead. There was a chain lingerie store there, and this time, Kelsey would make sure to leave on her sunglasses.

A half-hour later, Kelsey walked across the skybridge, a pink-and-black-striped bag tucked neatly in the bottom of her tote bag. She had found a few things, but after looking had decided that she would just order the rest online. As she stepped off the skybridge and into the department store, Kelsey realized that she had one more purchase to make. It was time to replace the Chanel lipstick that Jessica had brought her from Paris.

Kelsey rode the escalators down to the first floor, deliberately passing by the lingerie department, and glancing over at the designer gowns as she rode by. Summer was almost over, and by the time they returned home from their Italian honeymoon, the social season in Seattle would be in full swing. And as the new Mrs. Tyler Olsen, Kelsey had a feeling that she would soon be wearing some of the gowns that now sparkled on the racks.

She reached the first floor, glanced at the new autumn shoes, and headed towards the cosmetics department. But as she passed by the fine jewelry area, something caught her eye.

Kelsey stopped and looked into one of the glass cases. Sitting in pride of place was a stunning gold cuff bracelet. It was beautiful, with broad golden strands criss-crossing the bold gold frame.

"May I help you?" the salesman asked.

And to Kelsey's own surprise, she said as she pointed at the bracelet,

"I'd like to try this on."

A few moments later, Kelsey's tote bag was propped in a soft chair, while Kelsey looked at the bracelet on her arm. It was just as stunning in person, but there was just one problem. It was too big for Kelsey. It fit, but the piece was clearly not designed for her. The cuff felt almost overwhelming on Kelsey's arm. She was tall, but not so tall to be able to carry off such a bold piece.

Kelsey looked at the cuff in disappointment. In addition to how much she liked the jewelry visually, it also had an additional benefit. It was expensive, and since she was now carrying the cards that Tyler had given her, such a large purchase would show him that she was taking his request to spend his money seriously. Kelsey gently began to remove the cuff, but as she did so, a thought came to her.

"Shall I wrap this up for you?" the salesman asked.

"Actually, I'd like you to send it to San Francisco," Kelsey replied.

A while later, Kelsey sat happily at her desk at work. Morgan's birthday gift was on its way to her, and Kelsey was thrilled. Jessica had bought so many nice things for Kelsey, and it was nice to have the opportunity to pay it forward. Kelsey knew that not only would the cuff look great on Morgan, but Morgan would also love it. Perhaps she would love it even more, now that Morgan wasn't dating her own billionaire.

Now that Morgan's birthday gift was taken care of, the only thing besides work that Kelsey needed to do before they left, was to order her honeymoon lingerie. As she scrolled through various websites at her desk, she wondered what Tyler would like.

A part of her was surprised that Tyler liked her in lingerie. Tyler was often so serious, so down-to-earth, that before she had got married, Kelsey had wondered if he would. But when they had been in Vancouver, Kelsey had discovered that Tyler was a bit of a connoisseur.

He liked her in black and deep, rich colors, because he always complimented her when she wore them. Whenever Kelsey wore a piece with strings or laces, Tyler invariably spent a minute tugging at them, unlacing them, or undoing their bows. For her part, although Tyler always made her feel special, Kelsey liked getting dressed up for him. It made her feel like a woman, with desires of her own.

Kelsey found a British website that she liked, but paused at the thought that the pieces might not get to her in time. She clicked over to the shipping, then laughed to herself. She could afford to have anything she wanted sent next-day air.

Although she had saved her personal credit card in her tablet, she hadn't yet put in the number for her new black card. She pulled the new credit card out of her wallet and set it on the desk. She pondered what Tyler had said. The thought of having a credit card that she could buy a car with was difficult to process. But at the moment, she was only buying a couple of hundred dollars' worth of lingerie.

Only. Kelsey smiled to herself. How things had changed in a few months. A year earlier, and Kelsey would have balked at paying thirty dollars for a bra. Particularly because with her small bust, she really didn't need one.

Kelsey stopped abruptly when she read the first line on her tablet. She had no idea what the billing address of the card was. Nor did she have a clue where things were supposed to be shipped. Tyler had said that everything was sent to Tactec, but Kelsey had no idea what that meant.

Kelsey thought for a moment. Of course she could message Tyler at work and ask, but it seemed like too much trouble. The same went for Jeffrey. Jess ordered online all the time, but her accounts were managed by Bob's secretary Carol. Kelsey tapped her tablet and clicked 'Pay using saved card'. The black card's first online purchase would have to wait for another day.

"So what did you buy?" Tyler asked Kelsey when he picked her up at work that night.

"Are you spying on me?"

Tyler grinned. "I told Jeffrey to tell me the minute you bought something with one of the cards." he replied.

"I bought Morgan's birthday gift," Kelsey reported.

Tyler pouted. "I thought you were buying something for me."

"I did that too," Kelsey said. "But I have a question for you. How do I order things online? I mean, what address do I use?"

"I'll message it to you. Billing address and phone number are David Sheinman's office, and I usually have things shipped to Jeffrey's desk at Tactec."

"OK, thanks. Because I didn't have the addresses, I did have to pay for something myself."

"Reimburse yourself from the ATM," Tyler replied.

Kelsey frowned.

"What?" Tyler challenged her.

"Never mind."

"Good," Tyler said with a smile. "So what did you buy for me?"

"You'll see."

"Tonight?" Tyler said hopefully.

"It's being shipped."

"This weekend?"

"You'll see it in Italy."

"I don't want to wait that long," Tyler pouted.

"I have other things to show you before then," Kelsey replied seductively.

"I hope so," Tyler said, kissing her hand.

Kelsey was frantic. Bill had dumped two new clients on her desk, with the expectation that she would get started on their projects this week, and in the meantime, she already had plenty of work of her own. She could have asked Jake to help, but since he was going to be the only full-time Intellectual Property lawyer in the office while she was away, Kelsey was trying to give him a break now.

Tiana and Dirk were still in the office, which was great, but they had projects of their own to finish. It was their final week in the Simon and Associates office, and the scheduled end of their internships, which meant that Kelsey had won the betting pool.

Millie stuck her head into Kelsey's office.

"Don't forget that you have a meeting with Bill and Dave Linden in ten minutes," Millie said brightly. Millie had been walking around the office like she was on cloud nine ever since Tori's brother had asked her out.

"Thanks," Kelsey said, and Millie walked on. Kelsey turned to her computer to pull up her notes for the meeting, but her eyes glanced at her phone first. Tyler had sent her a message.

Wishing that my beautiful bride was here in my arms. I love you, It read.

Kelsey stopped, and picked up her phone.

I wish I was too. I love you, she wrote. And with a sigh, she put the phone down and got back to work.

Kelsey was able to put her hectic week on pause briefly on Thursday, when she and Jake took Tiana and Dirk out to lunch at Chapin's.

"Anything you want," Jake said when they received their menus. "It's on Kelsey."

Kelsey laughed. "That's fine. I'll pick up the bill."

The group placed their orders, then as the waitress walked away, Tiana turned to Kelsey.

"Kelsey, I have a question for you. Why did you come work for Bill Simon?"

"Why do you ask?" Jake intervened. After Devin's accusations, Kelsey felt that Jake had become a little protective of her.

"Bill Simon offered me a full-time job when I graduate," Tiana said, and she seemed surprised as she did. "But I'm wondering whether to take it."

Jake clearly had an opinion, as 'no' was written all over his face, but he remained silent.

"What's your hesitation?" Kelsey asked.

"Besides Bill's crazy?" Dirk piped in.

"Besides that," Jake said.

"I think that's the main one," Tiana admitted.

"Do you have any other offers?"

"Not yet," Tiana said.

"Does Bill want a response now?" Kelsey asked.

"No," Tiana said. "He said that if I wanted to come back, just let him know next summer and that he would make room for me in the IP department."

"Why don't you just apply to a few other firms then, and see what kinds of offers you get?" Jake said.

"Jake has a point. You know what Bill's like to work for, so you would know what to expect if you came back," Kelsey said as the waitress brought over their drinks.

"Will you still be here?" Tiana asked Kelsey.

Kelsey thought for a moment.

"Probably," she said.

"That took a little too long," Jake commented.

"It's not only up to me, Jake. I'm married to Tyler, so my life is a bit more complicated now," Kelsey said.

Jake laughed. "Since Tyler can't pry his mother away from Bill Simon, he's going to at least get his new wife back?"

Kelsey grinned. "Something like that," she admitted. "No, I'm pretty sure I'll still be here."

"Well, if I still have you as my mentor, I wouldn't mind coming back," Tiana said. "I learned a lot this summer from you."

"I'm glad to hear that," Kelsey said, beaming.

"Me, too," Dirk said. "But I think I can only handle one summer with Bill Simon."

"That's fine. Some people can only handle one day," Jake replied with a smile.

"Do you think she'll come back?" Jake asked Kelsey. They had returned from a long and expensive lunch. Kelsey didn't mind paying for it. Thanks to the summer associates' help, she had had more time off than she had expected during the summer.

"I don't know."

"Yeah, once she recovers from this summer, she'll probably come to her senses and start sending out resumes," Jake said.

"You're still here," Kelsey pointed out.

"I have a family to support. What's your excuse?"

"I like it."

Jake laughed. "Right. Let's see if you come back after three weeks in Italy with your billionaire husband. You'll come to your senses too."

Kelsey giggled. "Maybe," she admitted.

"It was nice knowing you," Jake joked, giving Kelsey a wave and heading for his office.

"I'll send you a postcard," Kelsey called after him.

Kelsey's phone beeped with a notification. She glanced at it, and noticed that it was from Jess, addressed to the Line group that included herself, Tyler, and Ryan. Kelsey's eyes widened when she saw the picture attached to Jessica's message.

It was a photograph of Bob's yacht, the *Yulia*. On the deck, there were at least a half-dozen beautiful, bikini-clad women, in addition to the lone man.

Bob Perkins.

Jessica's message read, *My father-in-law…. Sigh.*

Ryan replied, *I'm glad that Bob's having fun.*

Kelsey turned away from the phone. She wasn't sure what to think, and she certainly had nothing to say.

The phone beeped with another notification, and Kelsey glanced back down. There was a message from Tyler, this time directly to Kelsey, and not to the group.

I guess Bob wanted to send a message to someone, Tyler wrote.

Kelsey picked up her phone and wrote, *What do you mean?*

Tyler replied, *Bob allowed that photo to be taken. There's no way paparazzi would have gotten that close to the boat otherwise.*

Kelsey turned away from the phone again. She realized that Tyler was right, and she was sure she knew exactly who the message was meant for.

"Eighty, ninety," Tori counted.

"Come on, Tori," Jake said.

"One hundred, one ten, and one twenty," Tori said, counting the rest of the money out onto the reception desk.

"Thanks," Kelsey said. She thought for a moment. "I thought only eleven people were in the pool."

"Your husband was in the office and bet against you," Tori said, laughing.

"Tyler's in trouble," Millie said joyfully.

"I don't mind. Now his ten dollars is mine," Kelsey said, picking up the stack of ten-dollar bills.

"Now you just have to figure out how to get the other two billion," Tori said.

"I'll think about it this weekend," Kelsey said.

"Speaking of, thank your mother-in-law. This is the first Labor Day I've had off since I've worked here," Marie said to Kelsey.

"I'll try to remember," Kelsey said. Tactec was closed on Labor Day, so Lisa Olsen had talked Bill into taking a long weekend with her.

"So what are you doing with the money?" Millie asked Kelsey.

"I told Tyler that I would take him out to dinner," Kelsey said.

"I can't believe that you won," Tori mused. "And you're going to win the next pool."

"Really?" Kelsey said excitedly.

"It's August 31st, and we still have new associates," Tori shrugged. "No one else thought they would last past the 25th."

"When do I get paid?" Kelsey asked.

"Spoken like a true Olsen," Tori teased. "Raj will give you the money on Tuesday. He's in charge of that pool."

"Great," Kelsey said happily.

"Does that mean that Tyler gets dinner twice?" Millie asked.

"I don't know," Kelsey said. "Tori, did Tyler bet against me?"

"I think I have work to do," Tori said with a grin.

As Kelsey was standing outside of her building waiting for Tyler, her phone rang. She glanced at the name in surprise, then picked up.

"Hi, Zach."

"Hi, Mrs. Olsen," Zach said. "It's been a while."

"It has. How are you?"

Zach gave a deep sigh. "Kels, I need you to throw Tyler out."

"What?"

"Just for the night. Ask Jess to go out with you or something."

"Why?"

"I need to talk to Tyler, but every time I ask him to come over to the Eastside he tells me that if the choice is between seeing me and staying at home with you, there's no contest. I haven't seen him in weeks."

Kelsey laughed. "Do you need to see him before we leave?" she asked.

"Yeah, I kind of do," Zach said.

Kelsey thought. Erica had given Kelsey a standing invitation to visit on Saturday afternoons because Marquis had soccer practice then, and Erica didn't like to watch.

"I'll talk to him tonight," Kelsey said. "You're free tomorrow?"

"I'm free whenever," Zach said. "Thanks, Kels."

"Any time," Kelsey said, and she hung up the phone. She sent a message to Erica, who replied instantly that she was free and that Kelsey should come over and hang out. Just as she sent her goodbye message to Erica, Tyler walked up.

"Hi, beautiful," he said, kissing her.

"Hi, Tyler," Kelsey said happily.

Tyler put his arm around Kelsey's shoulder. "So where are you taking me?" he asked.

"I heard that you bet against me," Kelsey replied with mock anger.

"I was simply hedging our bets," Tyler said innocently. "In case you didn't win."

Kelsey giggled. "Good save," she commented.

"Thank you," Tyler said with a grin. "So where are we going?"

"You'll see," Kelsey said.

She led him a couple of blocks away to a new American-cuisine restaurant that had opened. They walked in and sat in a cozy booth. Tyler held Kelsey's hands across the table once they had ordered.

"So, I'm going to see Erica tomorrow afternoon," Kelsey said. "I'll go straight from work."

Tyler frowned. "Zach got to you," he said.

Kelsey wasn't sure what she was supposed to say. "Erica invited me a long time ago."

"But for some reason, you need to go tomorrow?" Tyler replied.

"OK, fine. Zach called me."

Tyler sighed. "Kelsey."

"Tyler, Zach's your best friend. You should spend time with him occasionally."

"I only want to spend time with you."

"I know. Zach told me. But you shouldn't have told him that."

"Why? It's the truth."

"It probably hurt Zach's feelings," Kelsey said.

"Zachary doesn't have any feelings to hurt," Tyler retorted. "Anyway, Zach doesn't want anything important."

"He said he needed to talk to you."

"He doesn't," Tyler said, kissing Kelsey's hand.

"Go anyway," Kelsey said. "I'll bring you some bread home. Erica said that we'll bake at her house tomorrow."

"I'll go, but I'm doing it for you."

"OK, Tyler," Kelsey said with a giggle.

The next day, Kelsey was sitting at her desk at work finishing things up before she headed over to Erica's apartment on Beacon Hill. Her phone buzzed with a notification, and she looked at it and laughed. Tyler had sent her a picture of Zach and himself sitting in a restaurant. Tyler was frowning.

At 2 p.m., Kelsey drove over to Erica's house, and Erica greeted her happily.

"Kelsey!" Erica said, giving her a warm hug. "It's so good to see you.

Come in."

Kelsey walked into the small apartment, a housewarming gift in her hands. Kelsey looked around in interest. The last time she could remember being in an apartment this small was her own in Greenwood over a year ago. Kelsey realized that her sense of perspective was changing because she was married to Tyler. It wasn't surprising, but it felt a little strange.

"Thank you. This is for you."

"Thanks, Kelsey," Erica said, taking the gift. "How are you? How's married life?"

"It's great," Kelsey said.

"Should I open this now?" Erica asked.

"You should. I was hoping we could use it today," Kelsey replied.

"Now I'm really interested," Erica said, setting the package down on the kitchen table, which was right next to the front door. Kelsey stood next to the refrigerator as Erica looked for a pair of scissors. Kelsey glanced at the door of the refrigerator, where there were several photographs and notes. Suddenly one of them caught her eye. It was on expensive notepaper, and the name on the top line was *Kelsey Olsen*.

As Erica opened the packaging and chatted, Kelsey attempted to read the handwritten note without Erica noticing. It was a thank-you note for a pizza stone, that seemingly had been Erica and Marquis' gift to the Olsens. The note gushed about how wonderful the gift was, how the couple couldn't wait to use it, and how thoughtful the gift had been.

In the meantime, Kelsey had never seen a pizza stone anywhere in her house. In fact, she wasn't sure that she had seen any wedding gifts at all.

"Oh, Kelsey, these are beautiful!" Erica said. Kelsey had brought Erica a set of blue-striped bowls that she had thought would be nice when baking. "Thank you so much."

"You're welcome."

"We should definitely use these today," Erica said. "I know you like to bake too. Have you had a chance to use your wedding gift yet?"

Kelsey shook her head. "Not yet, but I hope to make pizza for Tyler soon," she said, breathing a sigh of relief for the note.

"The crust will come out perfect," Erica said breezily. "Just make sure it's super hot before you put the dough on it."

"I'll do that," Kelsey replied.

They spent the afternoon making quick breads and chatting. It turned out that Erica baked bread every weekend, so by the time Kelsey left, she was not only carrying two loaves of chocolate-vanilla-swirl bread, but also had two loaves of artisan rosemary bread that Erica had started in her bread maker before Kelsey had arrived. Kelsey was amused to hear that Erica had used her own pizza stone to bake them.

Kelsey was cutting a slice from the chocolate-vanilla-swirl bread when she heard Tyler's keys in the door.

"Tyler!" she said happily, setting down her knife and running over to greet him.

"Princess," Tyler said, taking her into his arms.

"How was your day?" she asked.

"Miserable," Tyler replied.

"It was not," Kelsey pouted.

"It was. I had to spend all day listening to Zach talk about his new girlfriend."

"Is it serious?" Kelsey asked Tyler.

"I hope not, for her sake."

"I thought you were his friend," Kelsey scolded.

"I've known Zach longer than I've known almost anyone. I'm just being honest," Tyler replied.

"Come have some chocolate bread," Kelsey said, taking his hand and guiding him to the kitchen.

"How's Erica?" Tyler asked, as Kelsey handed him a piece of bread.

"She's good. We spent the afternoon baking."

"You made this?" Tyler asked, taking a large bite.

Kelsey nodded, and cut another piece for herself. "I did."

"Mrs. Olsen, cooking for her husband," Tyler teased.

"Funny," Kelsey said.

"It's delicious," Tyler said.

"Thanks. So when I was at Erica's today, there was a thank-you note on her refrigerator door for the wedding gift they gave us."

Tyler looked at Kelsey as he chewed.

"It was from me," Kelsey said. "But I didn't write a thank-you note. And I never saw their gift."

"OK," Tyler said.

"That doesn't strike you as odd?"

"No," Tyler replied.

Kelsey narrowed her eyes at him. "Clearly I'm missing something," she said, leaning against the counter.

"I don't write my own thank-you notes. Jeffrey writes them," Tyler said.

"In your name."

"Of course."

"Of course?"

"Kels, we probably received thousands of wedding gifts. I'm guessing that you didn't have time to write thousands of thank-you notes. So Jeffrey probably arranged someone to write them for you."

"I guess," Kelsey said and she accepted the logic behind Tyler's words. "But since I didn't write them, I also don't know what we got."

"Did you want something?" Tyler asked, taking another bite of bread.

"No, it's not that. It's just that Erica expected me to know what she had given us, and I didn't have a clue. I would have been in real trouble if she hadn't put the thank-you note on the refrigerator door."

"I'm sure there's a list somewhere," Tyler said. "Jeffrey will know."

"So you don't know what we got either?" Kelsey asked.

"My godfather gave us an island," Tyler said.

"An island?" Kelsey said in surprise.

"A small one. In the San Juans."

"We own an island in the San Juans?" Kelsey said in disbelief.

"It will take millions to develop. We can go camping on it sometime if you want, though," Tyler replied.

"Who is your godfather?" Kelsey asked.

"Jon Lane," Tyler said, breaking off a piece of bread and putting it in his mouth.

"Jon Lane? The Jon Lane?" Kelsey said. Jon Lane was another legend in the tech industry, having developed one of the best-known and most secure electronic payment systems.

"Lisa went to college with him," Tyler replied. "You saw him at the wedding."

"I didn't know he was your godfather." Kelsey said.

"He is. Can I have another slice?"

"Of course," Kelsey said. Tyler walked over to the kitchen and cut another slice of bread.

"Do you have one godfather or two?"

"Two," Tyler replied between bites of bread.

"Who's the other?"

"Max Ruiz. He's a painter in New Mexico. One of Chris's friends. He sent us one of his paintings."

"Godmother?"

"Keiko Payne."

"Interesting."

"Not particularly," Tyler said, taking a bite of bread.

"I think so," Kelsey mused. "Is Lisa Zach's godmother?"

"No. Andrew's sister is."

"I learned something new today," Kelsey said. "So Jeffrey has the list of wedding presents? Is there anything else interesting on it?"

Tyler shook his head. "I don't remember. I think someone gave us a boat."

"A boat?"

"A yacht, really. And a couple of cars. That's all I can remember. No, wait, Jeffrey said there's some gems for you."

"Gems?"

"He said that they needed to have them appraised for insurance before they were set in a necklace. I'm sure he'll mention it to you."

"You're joking with me, right?"

"Why would I be joking?" Tyler asked, eating his bread.

"I guess you wouldn't. Someone gave us a yacht? Where is it?"

"I don't know where the yacht is, but everything else is in a warehouse in Kent."

"A warehouse?"

"Gifts that come in are sent to the warehouse," Tyler explained. "They are photographed, cataloged, and a thank-you note is sent out. Every few months Camille goes to the warehouse, determines which gifts, if any, are kept, and the rest are quietly donated to charity."

"Gifts? What other gifts?"

"Lisa gets birthday gifts from lots of people, and tons of holiday gifts show up between Thanksgiving and Christmas. And the twins' gifts are there now, too."

"The twins?"

"Hundreds of Tactec employees sent presents to them, from all over the world. Plus all of Ryan and Bob's friends. And suppliers, people who want to get on Bob's good side. There's thousands of gifts at the warehouse."

"I had no idea," Kelsey said. She thought for a moment. "But when the Hudson family sent you and Ryan snacks at law school they came directly to you."

Tyler shrugged. "They knew where we were."

"So when we have kids, strangers will send them gifts?"

"Probably," Tyler said.

"And they'll get personalized thank-you notes with my name on them."

"Yes."

"That's really odd."

"When you put it like that, it is," Tyler said.

"Wait, so did we get wedding gifts from strangers?"

"We might have. We definitely got gifts from people who weren't at the wedding."

"So when I'm back in Port Townsend, people might come up to me and expect that I know what they gave me for our wedding because I wrote them a thank-you note?"

"Could be."

Kelsey munched on her piece of bread.

"I guess I'd better get that list from Jeffrey," she said.

Kelsey and Tyler spent a quiet Sunday and Monday together. They lay in bed, went on long, leisurely walks, and just enjoyed each other's company. Late on Monday night, as Tyler read his Kindle next to her, Kelsey glanced at her Instagram feed. Unlike the one that Becks had set up for her, this one was private, and Kelsey never posted on it, but instead used it to keep up with friends and family.

Morgan had written Kelsey a message, thanking her for the bracelet, and telling her that she would post a picture of herself wearing it on Instagram. Morgan had been posting on Instagram a lot lately, mostly pictures from the over the top parties that she worked on. Today's post was just a little different.

Morgan was sitting on a bar stool, in what looked like a hip Spanish restaurant. The gold cuff bracelet that Kelsey had sent her was prominent on Morgan's arm.

Kelsey beamed. The bracelet looked great on Morgan, just as she expected it would. But as she looked closer, Kelsey realized that the picture wasn't just meant for her.

In addition to the beautiful bracelet, and the elegant looking Morgan, there was a man, who wasn't completely visible, hand feeding a piece of tapas to Morgan.

The caption read simply,

Happy birthday to me.

"Interesting," Kelsey said.

"What's interesting?" Tyler asked Kelsey. She showed him the photo. "Morgan has a new boyfriend?" he asked.

"I don't know," Kelsey replied.

"I guess she saw the photos of Bob," Tyler commented.

"Do you think so?"

"Come on. Spanish restaurant on her birthday? Morgan's not subtle. This was meant for Bob."

"Yeah, I guess you're right," Kelsey agreed. Tyler went back to his book, and Kelsey sent a message to Morgan.

I saw your Instagram, Kelsey wrote.

Thanks again for the bracelet! I love it, Morgan replied.

Do you have a new boyfriend? Kelsey wrote. She had known Morgan forever. There was no reason not to get straight to her question.

You won't tell anyone?

No, Kelsey replied.

No, the guy in the picture was my friend Dale. His boyfriend took the picture, Morgan replied.

OK, keep me posted. Have a great birthday, Kelsey said, and she signed off.

On Tuesday, Jessica met Kelsey downtown for lunch. Dr. Hunter had returned to New York, and for the first time in over a month, Jessica was free to leave home.

"How is your mom? Did everything work out OK?" Kelsey asked as they sat at their table. Jessica placed her designer handbag in the chair next to her.

Jess looked a little confused, like she couldn't believe what she was about to say.

"Joey picked her up at the airport, drove her home, and when they got there, she discovered the locks on the house had been changed."

"No," Kelsey said in disbelief.

"So Joey drove her to his house."

"What did your father say?" Kelsey asked. She couldn't believe that Jessica's father had locked his own wife — the mother of his children — out of her house.

"Well, Mom went to work on Tuesday, and discovered my father was no longer speaking to her. About anything at all. If he has something to say about the dental office, he either tells the office manager or sends her an email."

Kelsey didn't verbalize what she was thinking, but Jessica did.

"He's crazy," Jessica said.

"What's your mom going to do?" Kelsey asked.

"Well, she and Joey are going to go back this weekend, call a locksmith, and remove her things. Then she's going to temporarily move in with Joey."

"Temporarily?" Kelsey asked.

"Kels, I don't know," Jessica said in defeat. "I have no idea what she's going to do. I told her if she needed anything to let me know, but Mom said that business is fine, and Daddy doesn't have control over her finances. They've always run the business as a partnership for tax reasons, so Mom is OK financially. I just… I don't know what to do."

"What can you do?" Kelsey asked.

"Exactly. Nothing," Jessica replied.

"It will work out, Jess," Kelsey said.

"I hope so," Jessica said. "I just don't know what working out actually means. Is Mom going to live with Joey forever? Will Daddy get sick of cooking for himself and let her come back? Does she want to go back? I have no idea."

"Sorry, Jess," Kelsey said. She could sense Jessica's frustration, but — as was true for Jess — there was nothing that she could do.

"It's OK," Jessica said. "Let me tell you what I want you to buy for me in Italy."

Kelsey worked non-stop on Wednesday and Thursday, eating dinner at her desk both nights. Finally, just before midnight on Thursday night, Kelsey turned out the light in her office and let Tyler escort her home.

"Happy anniversary, Kelsey," Tyler said on Friday morning, kissing Kelsey on the nose.

Kelsey opened her eyes sleepily and looked into Tyler's sparkling-brown eyes.

"Happy anniversary, Tyler."

Tyler pulled Kelsey closer, and Kelsey snuggled into his strong arms. She felt at peace and loved.

"Should we go to Italy today?" Tyler asked.

Kelsey giggled. "I think we should," she replied.

Tyler kissed her hair. "Do you want coffee?" he asked.

"I think so. It's going to be a long day," Kelsey replied.

Twenty minutes later, Kelsey was drying her wet hair with a soft white towel. Jeffrey had arrived a few minutes earlier, accompanied by Conor, and the two of them were talking to Tyler in the living room. Conor would not be accompanying them on the trip, but he had made security arrangements for them, and Kelsey assumed that he was briefing Tyler on those arrangements.

Kelsey looked at herself in the mirror. Although at first glance her outfit seemed casual, it had actually been meticulously curated by Jeffrey. Black jeans, designer slip-on sneakers, a heather-gray cashmere sweatshirt, layered over a sexy black tank. Kelsey looked runway ready. But despite the fact that the only runway she would see today was the one at the airport, she knew — as did Jeffrey — that Mrs. Tyler Olsen would be seen by everyone else. And today she needed to dress the part.

Kelsey's bags had been similarly upgraded. Gone was her beloved travel backpack that she had slung over her shoulder for many trips with Tyler. Instead, she had a brand new black Rimowa suitcase, with a large black leather tote for her tablet. Diamond studs in her ears, her Cartier Tank watch on her wrist, and of course, most importantly, her wedding ring on her finger, Kelsey was ready to walk through New York City's busiest airport and through the paparazzi that lingered there.

Kelsey put her now slightly-damp hair into a neat top knot, and secured it with a gold ponytail holder. A bit of lip gloss, which she knew would be gone by the time they reached Seattle's airport, thanks to Tyler's kisses, and Kelsey was ready to go. She left the master bathroom and walked out into the living room.

"Good morning, Kelsey," Conor said brightly.

"Hi, Kelsey," Jeffrey said.

"Hi," Kelsey replied in greeting, a little distractedly, because from the corner of her eye, she could see that Tyler was frowning. Kelsey though that she knew why. She suspected that Conor's security arrangements didn't fit Tyler's plans.

"Are you ready to go, beautiful?" Tyler asked her. Kelsey blushed at his words, but she nodded. She picked up her new tote.

"We are allowed to leave?" Tyler asked Conor pointedly. Kelsey knew from his tone that her suspicions were correct.

"Stay out of trouble. No one wants to fly to Italy to rescue you," Conor said in reply.

"We'll be fine," Tyler replied.

"Kelsey, I've forwarded the list of things that the two of you are not allowed to do while you're in Italy. Make sure that Tyler doesn't do any of them," Conor said to Kelsey.

Intimidated by his forceful look, Kelsey meekly said, "I'll see what I can do."

"No, she won't," Tyler said firmly.

"I'm warning you, Tyler," Conor said. Tyler shrugged unconcernedly.

"We need to go," Jeffrey said, ending the standoff. "We have a plane to catch."

"You're sitting in coach, right?" Tyler asked.

"Business. Don't worry, I'll be far away from the two of you," Jeffrey said with a grin.

"I hope so," Tyler replied.

Kelsey was trying not to laugh. Between Conor's rules, and the fact that

Jeffrey was tagging along on their honeymoon, it was clear that Tyler wasn't having a good morning.

"Let's go," Kelsey said peacefully, taking Tyler's hand into her own. Tyler smiled at her, and gave her hand a gentle squeeze.

"The luggage has been taken downstairs," Jeffrey said to Kelsey as she and Tyler followed him out of the apartment.

"I'll lock up. Have a good trip," Conor said.

"Bye, Conor," Kelsey said as the apartment door closed behind them.

Kelsey looked at Tyler's clothing as they waited for the elevator. His look had also been subtly changed, although not as much as Kelsey's own. He too was wearing a cashmere sweater, although his was navy. At the moment, it was casually draped over his broad shoulders.

"Breakfast is in the car for you, Kelsey," Jeffrey said.

"I, on the other hand, am getting nothing," Tyler commented as the elevator arrived. The group of three got on, and Jeffrey tapped the button for the lobby.

"Margaret is upset with you after your little stunt last weekend," Jeffrey said. Kelsey looked at Tyler, who looked back at Jeffrey with innocent eyes.

"Stunt? I needed Lisa's help."

"In the middle of the afternoon? On a Saturday? When you knew that Bill Simon was with her?" Jeffrey said.

"Lisa said that her door is always open. Anyway, she bothers me whenever she feels like it," Tyler replied unapologetically.

"I'm not taking sides," Jeffrey replied. "But that's why there's nothing in the car for you."

"I know how to stop at McDonald's," Tyler said. "Make sure you tell Margaret that's where I ate because she didn't pack me anything."

"Tyler, you should really work harder at getting along with your family," Jeffrey said as the doors of the elevator opened and they walked out into the lobby.

"I get along with everyone fine," Tyler replied. "Bill Simon's not my family, so I don't need to let him get in the way of speaking to my mother."

Jeffrey gave Tyler a hard look as they headed out to the car.

"Tyler, everyone — including Bill —knows that you aren't happy about their relationship. You don't need to spend your weekends trying to sabotage it."

Tyler stopped at the side of the car. "I needed to speak to the CEO. It isn't my fault that she dropped everything to deal with my question."

"You knew she would," Jeffrey said.

"We're done now," Tyler said dismissively.

"Fine," Jeffrey said. "But you only get one family, Tyler. One mother and one father. Learn to appreciate them."

"I do. Can we get in the car now?"

"Yes, the lecture is over," Jeffrey said.

"Good," Tyler said, opening the car door for Kelsey. She got in, and Tyler followed her inside. Jeffrey got into the front.

"Good morning, Kelsey."

"Hi, Martin," Kelsey replied, but she was looking at her husband, who didn't seem happy. Tyler glanced at her, and handed her the bag that was hanging on the back of the seat.

"This is for you," he commented.

"I'll share," Kelsey replied.

Tyler shook his head. "I'll eat at the airport," he said, looking out of the window.

As they pulled away from the curb, Kelsey took Tyler's hand and leaned her head against his shoulder.

"Quite a start to our honeymoon," she noted.

Tyler chuckled.

"I'm sure it will improve," he said, leaning his head onto hers. He lifted her hand and kissed it.

"What happened on Saturday?" Kelsey asked.

"Nothing important," Tyler replied.

"No?"

"No. I don't want to talk about work," Tyler said firmly. "We're on our honeymoon."

"OK," Kelsey said, closing her eyes. At this moment, she felt a little bad for Tyler. Although he was an adult, he was surrounded by people who had known him since he was a child, and who all felt entitled to regulate his behavior. She imagined it was frustrating for him. So even though she was curious, she decided not to press him on what had happened over the weekend. She would trust that he would tell her if it was important.

"You don't want to eat?" Tyler asked.

"Not if you don't," Kelsey replied.

"You should eat, Kels," Tyler said. "It's probably still warm."

Tyler lifted his head from hers.

"Go ahead. You can sneak me a bite," he commented.

"All right," Kelsey said, opening her eyes, and sitting up. She lifted the bag up and put it in her lap. A folded note sat on top, and Kelsey pulled it out. Tyler gently took it from her fingers.

"I'll read it," Tyler said. "See what's inside."

Kelsey looked inside the bag, and pulled out two sturdy cardboard containers with clear plastic tops. Inside one was a delicious-looking array of sliced breakfast breads, including blueberry-banana, cranberry-walnut, and a cinnamon swirl. In the other was an open-face sandwich. Kelsey didn't recognize the ingredients, but it looked amazing.

"What does the note say?" Kelsey asked.

"It says that you should enjoy your meal," Tyler said, dropping the note back into the empty bag.

"Do you want some?" Kelsey asked.

"Absolutely not," Tyler said.

"Why not?" Kelsey asked in surprise.

"Because Margaret deliberately made things I don't like," Tyler said.

"Really?" Kelsey asked, looking back at the food. "I thought you liked banana bread?"

"I don't like blueberries in bread," Tyler replied. "Or cinnamon bread. Or walnuts in almost anything."

"What about the sandwich?" Kelsey asked.

"It's smoked gouda on apple butter. I don't like that either," Tyler replied.

"Sorry," Kelsey said.

"It's OK. Eat. It will make Margaret happy," Tyler said. "Martin?"

"Mr. Olsen?" Martin replied.

"Stop at the next McDonald's," Tyler said.

A few minutes later, Tyler was breaking a piece off a McDonald's hash brown.

"Want some?" he asked Kelsey. She shook her head and took another bite of the smoked gouda sandwich. It was heaven.

Tyler popped the hash brown into his mouth.

Over Jeffrey's protests, they had not only stopped at McDonald's, but Tyler had also taken photos of the bag — and the lone hash brown inside — and sent them to both Margaret and Lisa.

Tyler broke off another piece of hash brown.

"Is it good?" Jeffrey asked sarcastically from the front.

"Delicious," Tyler said.

"Really?" Kelsey whispered to Tyler.

"No, but I'm hungry," Tyler whispered back. "I should have gotten two," he added, loud enough for Jeffrey to hear. Kelsey stifled a giggle, and Tyler winked at her.

Less than five minutes later, Martin pulled the car in front of the "Arrivals" section at Sea-Tac airport. Kelsey was puzzled for just a second, then smiled at his ingenuity. It was virtually empty, at a time when Kelsey was sure the departures area was busy.

Tyler wiped his fingers on a napkin and tossed it into the McDonald's bag, while Kelsey replaced the top on the sandwich container. She hadn't finished it, because it was so delicious that she wanted to savor every bite. Kelsey placed the bag with the food into the large black leather tote, and placed the tote over her shoulder.

With his hand on the door, Tyler said to Jeffrey,

"We're done, right? We won't see you in Italy?"

"You'll probably see me board the plane," Jeffrey replied.

"I'll have my eyes closed," Tyler replied.

Martin burst out laughing from the driver's seat.

"Have a good trip, Kelsey." Jeffrey said. "I'll arrange for your bags to be delivered to the hotel in Rome."

"Thank you," Kelsey said, as Tyler opened the door of the town car, and she followed him out. He took her hand and swiftly led her into the terminal. Once they were inside, Tyler gave her a kiss on the lips.

"Let's get something to eat," he said.

About an hour later, Kelsey and Tyler boarded their plane. When she saw their seats, Kelsey frowned.

"We can't cuddle," she commented. The navy-blue first-class seats were staggered for privacy, each separated by a table. It was fine for business people, or those traveling alone, but not for honeymooners.

"That's why coach is more fun," Tyler commented. "Window or aisle?"

"Aisle," Kelsey said, and Tyler ducked into his seat. Kelsey put her black tote bag on the floor between them, and pulled out a soft black pashmina, which she draped over her legs. The plane was a little chilly already, probably since they were some of the first passengers to get on. Kelsey thought it might warm up once the plane was full. Tyler reached for her hand, and Kelsey took his. She turned the bright gold ring on his finger.

"Excited?" she asked.

"To be with you," Tyler replied, leaning over and giving her a kiss.

"Me too," Kelsey said. "I miss coach. I wish we could cuddle."

"I do too, but four hours into the flight you'll be happy to be in first class," Tyler said.

"Probably," Kelsey admitted. "So can I ask you a question?"

"You can ask me anything, Princess."

"Why does Martin call you 'Mr. Olsen'?"

Tyler sighed deeply. Kelsey was curious, because although she didn't know Martin well, she had seen him enough to know that he called Lisa and Bob by their first names. The last time Martin had addressed Kelsey directly, she had still been Miss North.

"It's a joke," Tyler said. "Martin's apartment over the garage used to be

61

my playroom, and I was moved out when he arrived. But I was upset that I had been moved out, so I kept going back. One day, Martin caught me there, and told me that it was his space now, and I wasn't allowed to play there anymore. And I told him that it wasn't his space, it was my mom's and since he worked for her, he needed to treat me nicely."

Kelsey laughed delightedly. She loved stories about Tyler as a little kid.

"Martin saluted me, said, 'Yes, Master Tyler', then threw me out of the room," Tyler continued.

"Master is only used as a title for little boys, right?"

"Right. Another reason Martin called me that for over fifteen years. I only graduated to Mr. Olsen when I married you."

"That's terrible," Kelsey giggled.

"What's terrible is that he won't stop."

"Actually, with all of the stories I've heard about you, I'm wondering if you were the terrible one. Not letting your parents sleep when you were a baby, arguing with the staff. I'm not sure I would have liked little Tyler Olsen," Kelsey commented.

"He took my space, Kelsey."

"I've seen Lisa's house. There are plenty of other places to play there."

"Whose side are you on?"

"Martin's," Kelsey replied with a smile.

Tyler pouted. He kissed her hand.

"Over the next three weeks I intend to change that," he said softly.

"Do you?" Kelsey asked. "How?"

Tyler smiled and his brown eyes sparkled. He kissed the palm of her hand and Kelsey felt a shiver of excitement at his look.

"One guess," Tyler said seductively.

"Excuse me," the stewardess said. "Can I get you a drink while we're waiting for the other passengers to board?"

"Cranberry juice, please," Kelsey said.

"Do you have ginger ale?" Tyler asked.

"Of course sir." the stewardess said. "I'll be right back."

"Ginger ale? Does your stomach hurt?"

"Let's just say that's my last visit to the golden arches for a while," Tyler commented.

"You aren't used to it," Kelsey commented.

"I don't recall you ordering anything," Tyler pointed out.

Kelsey giggled. "I've been dating you for a while. I'm not used to it either," she agreed.

"I actually used to eat there a lot when I worked in the gallery with Chris. It was close and open 24 hours a day. Plus I could afford it on my tiny salary."

"Chris didn't feed you?"

"Not at midnight when we were busy cataloging new works. Chris doesn't believe in eating after nine. He says it's unhealthy."

"Is it?" Kelsey asked, as the stewardess brought their drinks and set them on the mini-table between them.

"Thank you," Tyler said to the stewardess.

"I'll be back with the snack basket," she said brightly, as she walked off.

"Don't ask me what Chris thinks," Tyler continued. "I just know that he almost never eats before noon or after nine. I think it's some intermittent fasting thing."

"Your parents have strange eating habits," Kelsey said. She had never seen Lisa eat anything that wasn't meat, blueberries, or dessert.

"My parents are just strange," Tyler said, as the stewardess reappeared with the snack basket. Kelsey took out a strawberry-yogurt granola bar, while Tyler removed a package of chocolate cookies.

"Let me know if you need anything else," the stewardess said pleasantly. "We should be leaving soon."

"Thank you," Kelsey said as she left. Kelsey dropped the granola bar in her bag in case she wanted it later. She pulled the pashmina up higher.

"Are you cold?" Tyler asked.

"A little."

"I could warm you up," Tyler said.

"I bet you could. But not here."

"The restroom is right there," Tyler said, pointing.

"So?"

"We could join the mile-high club."

Kelsey blushed scarlet.

"No," she said firmly.

Tyler nuzzled her ear. "Are you sure? It would warm you up."

"Positive," Kelsey replied.

"The next time we're on a private plane..." Tyler said, letting the comment trail off.

"I'm not agreeing to anything, Counsel," Kelsey said.

"I bet I could talk you into it," Tyler whispered into her ear. Kelsey felt herself blush again. *Of course he could*, she thought. Tyler was irresistible to her.

"Don't," Kelsey said.

"We'll see," Tyler said. "Perhaps I'll try again when we're up in the air. You might want to be distracted during the flight."

"You're always distracting me, Mr. Olsen," Kelsey complained. Tyler laughed.

"I'm looking forward to three weeks of distracting each other," Tyler said, kissing her.

The flight to New York City was uneventful. Tyler held Kelsey's hand during takeoff and during the slight amount of turbulence the plane flew through. They ate the chicken-and-rice dish served at lunch, and the couple shared two packages of cookies during the flight. Kelsey also finished the delicious sandwich that Margaret had packed for her. Tyler, in the meantime, refused even one bite.

They watched two movies together, and Kelsey only charged her tablet, because the wifi was so slow. She and Tyler had told their respective bosses that they wouldn't be checking email while they were on vacation. Kelsey was confident that Bill wouldn't contact her unless necessary, Tyler less so about whether Lisa would contact him. Kelsey wasn't concerned though. She knew that Tyler didn't want their vacation to be interrupted, and that he would do everything he could to not work over the next three weeks.

The plane landed in New York on time, and they disembarked with the rest of the passengers. As promised, Jeffrey was nowhere to be seen. Kelsey held Tyler's hand tightly as he confidently led her through the terminal.

"We have two hours before our next flight, Princess," Tyler said. "Are you hungry?"

"A little," Kelsey said. The meal on the plane had been fine, but it had been almost four hours since they had eaten.

"Good. I have a surprise for you," Tyler said happily.

A few minutes later, Kelsey was looking delightedly at a menu. Tyler had brought her to a Chef Marcus Samuelsson restaurant in the terminal. When they had been in New York for the proxy fight, Kelsey had eaten and enjoyed a lot of the chef's food.

"You've been married to me for two months. So what am I going to order?" Tyler asked, his brown eyes sparkling behind his menu.

Kelsey looked at Tyler, then back at her own menu.

"Well," Kelsey thought out loud, "normally, I would expect you to order the all-day breakfast, particularly since your breakfast this morning wasn't so great." Tyler smiled at her. "But," Kelsey continued, "I think that you're going to order the blackened catfish with grits." Kelsey looked at Tyler to see if she was correct.

"Well done, Counsel," Tyler said. "That is exactly what I'm going to have."

"How about you? Have you been paying attention to the preferences of your wife of two months?"

A sexy grin crossed Tyler's face, and Kelsey blushed a little.

"I certainly hope she thinks so," Tyler replied.

"What am I ordering?" Kelsey said, changing the subject before she turned red.

Tyler looked back down at the menu.

"You seem to like to eat salmon when we're away from Seattle, because it reminds you of home," Tyler commented. "But we just left this morning, plus I'm going to order a smoked salmon bagel as an appetizer, so you're just going to eat that."

Tyler glanced at her and Kelsey smiled back. He was right — Kelsey invariably helped herself to anything that Tyler was eating.

"You're going to get the BBQ gouda burger," Tyler concluded.

"What?" Kelsey said, looking down at her menu. "I didn't see that."

Tyler laughed. "What were you going to order then?"

"I was going to get the chorizo quesadilla."

"We'll get it as an appetizer. Have the burger."

"I didn't know that I liked gouda cheese until this morning," Kelsey said. "I'll get the burger. Thank you for the suggestion. I guess you know me better than I thought."

"I want to know everything about you," Tyler said seductively.

"I think you're almost there," Kelsey replied, looking into his smoldering eyes. She turned away and shifted in her chair. Tyler smiled at her.

"So," Tyler asked casually, "do you think we'll leave our hotel room in Rome?"

"No," Kelsey said honestly, refusing to look at him, "I don't think we will."

Tyler sighed deeply and Kelsey finally looked up. Frustration was written all over his face.

"What?"

"If only there were a hotel in the airport," Tyler said.

Kelsey looked away again, blushing. "Don't tease me, Tyler."

"Tease you? Do you know how difficult it is to be out in public with you, when all I want to do is be in bed with you?" Tyler asked her.

"Yeah. I do," Kelsey said, and she looked at Tyler once more.

"Come sit next to me," Tyler said seductively.

"I don't think so," Kelsey replied. They were sitting at an open table, in the middle of the restaurant, and there was no privacy to be had.

"Trust me," Tyler whispered.

"I don't trust myself," Kelsey replied.

Tyler laughed. "OK, then." he said. He leaned back in his chair and signaled the waitress. "I guess I'll have to wait until we get to our hotel in Italy to have what I really want."

"You and me both."

"Is that a promise?" Tyler asked.

Kelsey didn't answer, as the waitress appeared at her side. The couple ordered, and the waitress took their menus away. Tyler turned back to Kelsey once the waitress had left.

"Yes?" Kelsey asked him. She knew she was blushing, and she was very warm from their conversation.

"Do you promise to give me what I want in Italy?" Tyler asked bluntly.

For a moment, Kelsey hesitated. The lawyer in her wanted to ask Tyler what he wanted, before she made any promises at all. But she looked at his smoldering brown eyes, and found herself nodding. She knew that she would give Tyler anything he wanted. All he had to do was ask.

"Yes," Kelsey whispered. Tyler reached across the table, and stroked Kelsey's face with his fingertips. Kelsey closed her eyes, and willed her heart to stop pounding. She was putty in his hands, and they both knew it.

"Then I'll be patient," Tyler said, withdrawing his hand.

Kelsey opened her eyes, and as she looked at her husband, she burned with desire.

"I hope I can be," Kelsey said out loud, to Tyler's visible surprise and to her own.

"I bet there's a hotel a few minutes away," Tyler commented. "We could leave the airport and come back later."

"We'd miss our flight."

"We could book another one," Tyler replied.

Kelsey hesitated. She knew Tyler was completely serious.

"No," she said, with a great deal of hesitation. "I'll wait until Rome."

"You're sure?"

"Positive. You'll distract me," she said, then she saw the look in his eyes. "You'll distract me from wanting to be in bed with you," she corrected.

"I'm not sure I can," Tyler admitted.

"You're going to try," Kelsey said firmly. She looked around. "You brought me to this nice restaurant. I'm positive there are other things in the terminal that will help us get our minds off sex."

Tyler looked doubtful.

"Oh, come on, Tyler!" Kelsey said in irritation, and Tyler laughed.

"OK, Mrs. Olsen," he finally said. "I'll try."

"You aren't trying very hard to get my mind off sex," Kelsey commented a while later. They had enjoyed a fabulous meal, and now they were standing inside of a lingerie store in the terminal.

"It was your idea to stop here," Tyler commented. Kelsey giggled. In fact, it had been her idea. She had seen the store, and as she had been for weeks, she was still looking for pretty lingerie to wear for her new husband.

"I'm interested in your opinion," Kelsey admitted. She had wanted to go inside the store with Tyler, and she still felt a little shy, but after their banter in the restaurant, she knew there was no reason to be.

"Are you going to try things on?" Tyler asked hopefully.

"No," Kelsey said firmly. "You'll have to use your imagination."

Tyler pouted, and Kelsey gave him a kiss on the lips.

"I could just surprise you," she said, "but I'm curious to know what you like."

"You know what I like," Tyler replied.

"Tyler," Kelsey scolded.

"Fine," Tyler said. "Red is pretty," he said.

"Do you like this?" Kelsey asked, pulling a short silky red robe off of a hanger. She slipped it on over her now bare arms. Tyler was holding her bag and her cashmere sweatshirt.

"It's beautiful," Tyler said. "But I think you're wearing too much clothing under it."

"Patience, Mr. Olsen," Kelsey said, shrugging off the robe, and draping it over her arm.

Tyler's brown eyes glanced around the store.

"That one," he said, and Kelsey's eyes followed his to an all-lace teddy that left nothing to the imagination.

Kelsey blushed for what seemed like the hundredth time in an hour.

"There's no mystery," she pointed out, as they walked over to the display. Tyler leaned down and kissed Kelsey's neck.

"I don't need mystery," Tyler commented. Kelsey took her size off the rack, and they walked on. A few more selections, and they checked out, Tyler paying the bill. They left the store and paused outside of it, so Kelsey could put her sweatshirt back on. Tyler set their bags, including the new pink-and-black-striped one, at his feet.

71

"So will you take me lingerie shopping again?" Tyler asked, as Kelsey pushed a stray blonde hair away from her face.

"If you'd like," she said.

"It would be an honor," Tyler replied.

"Why do you like me in lingerie?" Kelsey asked.

"I like you in my bed," Tyler replied.

"That's not an answer."

"It's like the gift wrapping on a present that you know the contents of, and have been waiting for. The wrapping slows you up and makes the anticipation of your gift that much sweeter."

Kelsey looked up at Tyler. She threw her arms around his neck and gave him a kiss on the lips.

"That was an excellent answer, Mr. Olsen."

"My college education is paying off," Tyler replied.

Kelsey giggled. "Do we have to head for the gate?" she asked. It was just about 10 p.m. — almost time for their flight to Rome.

"Soon," Tyler said, picking up their bags with one hand and taking Kelsey's hand with his other.

A half-hour later, Kelsey was sitting on Tyler's lap, her arms crossed.

"Sorry, Princess," he said, holding her around the waist and nuzzling her side.

"I'm not leaving until they make me," Kelsey said defiantly.

"Good," Tyler said, stroking her thigh.

Once again they were sitting in premium class, but to both their dismay, the seats were completely separated for privacy. Tyler's seat was in front of Kelsey's, but because of the seat configuration, they couldn't see each other.

Tyler had explained that although Jeffrey had tried, he had been unable to book any of the three sets of 'honeymoon' seats. These seats were next to each other so couples could travel together, and the seats were designed to be comfortable. Once on the plane, Tyler and Kelsey had spoken to the stewardess and offered to trade, but the other passengers had declined. Tyler had told Kelsey that he would sweeten the deal with money, if one of the couples would take it, but Kelsey had said no. The flight was long, but they would be asleep during most of it, and Kelsey was concerned that if the other passengers discovered who was making the offer, the price would be sky-high. They would just have to deal.

"I love you," Tyler said blissfully as he held her.

"I love you too, Tyler," Kelsey replied. She felt very cozy in his arms. Suddenly the seatbelt sign flashed on.

"No," Kelsey said glumly.

"Have sweet dreams," Tyler said, but he continued to hold her firmly in his arms. "I'll be dreaming of you."

Kelsey's first moments in Rome were a blur. She hadn't slept well on the plane, having been separated from Tyler, and the two of them made up for lost time together in the back of the private car that had met them at the airport. Enveloped in Tyler's kisses, Kelsey barely saw the view from the car windows.

Kelsey waited as Tyler checked them in, and was thrilled when, card keys in hand, he whisked her up to their room. She would have a chance to appreciate the Eternal City later.

They walked into their suite, which Kelsey barely registered, thanks to her jet lag, general tiredness, but mostly for her impatience to be with Tyler. Tyler dropped their travel bags on the floor, picked Kelsey up into his arms, and swiftly carried her into the bedroom.

Kelsey clung to him as he gently placed her onto the bed. She kissed him over and over, not wanting to let him go, but Tyler removed himself from her grasp. They had other business to attend to, and Kelsey knew that he felt the same longing she did. Kelsey slipped off her tank top, while Tyler unbuttoned her jeans. She lay back on the pillows as her husband tugged her pants down, caressing her thighs as he did so.

Kelsey's breathing was rapid as Tyler removed his own clothing. He was naked, she lay on the bed in her bra and panties, and as Kelsey reached out for her husband, and pulled him down on top of herself, Tyler said,

"Welcome to Rome."

Hours later, Kelsey's eyes fluttered open, and she yawned. Tyler's arm was around her waist, and he was cuddled against her naked back. She smiled to herself, and turned to him.

"Hi, beautiful," he said, kissing her. He opened his big brown eyes, and looked into Kelsey's.

"Hi," Kelsey said blissfully.

Tyler pulled her closer, and nuzzled her loose blonde hair. "Should we go out?" he asked.

"I want to stay right here," Kelsey replied.

"We're only here for a few days," Tyler said.

"Five days now, five days later. Plenty of time," Kelsey replied.

Tyler laughed. "It's our honeymoon. I want you to see Rome," he said.

"I can see Rome any time. I want to see my husband," Kelsey replied.

"I'll be with you when you're seeing Rome," Tyler replied.

Kelsey ran her hand gently over Tyler's chest. "Then maybe we can go out," she conceded.

"Did you have a good nap?" Tyler asked.

"I did. I sleep better with you next to me," Kelsey said.

Tyler nuzzled her neck. "I'm so glad to be here with you. I always miss you so much," he said. Kelsey understood exactly what he meant. In Seattle, it always felt like they were running around. Going to work, being social. Living the life expected of Mr. and Mrs. Tyler Olsen.

There was so rarely time to spend together, just the two of them. But now, they had three weeks where there was nothing to do, and nowhere to be but in each other's arms. It was magical, and Kelsey was determined to to make the most of it.

She looked around the room. "This is really nice," she said. "We have a suite?"

"We do," Tyler said, nuzzling her neck once more. "Do you want to look around?"

"Maybe. I need a kiss first, though," Kelsey replied.

"Just one?"

"*Da mi basia mille,*" Kelsey said, with a touch of sass.

Tyler laughed. "Your thousand kisses will have to wait. I want to show you Rome."

"I'll take a down payment," Kelsey said stroking Tyler's face. His beard brushed against her palm.

Tyler leaned in and gave her a kiss on her lips.

"There."

"One kiss isn't enough."

Tyler kissed her again.

"There. That's two."

"A down payment is usually ten or twenty percent, Mr. Olsen. Didn't you learn anything in law school?"

"I forgot that I was dealing with Kelsey Olsen, Esquire," Tyler said. He kissed her again. "That's three. You can't have any more," he teased.

"No?" Kelsey asked.

"I want to take you out," Tyler said in reply.

"I bet I can convince you to kiss me," Kelsey said. She pressed her warm body against his.

"I bet you can too," Tyler said. He kissed her again. "I give up. We'll go out later."

"Good," Kelsey said. "You were on number five," she said, puckering her lips.

Tyler ignored her gesture. "If I'm giving you a thousand kisses, I get to decide where they go," he said.

Kelsey thought about the thousand kisses she had given Tyler.

"I can accept those terms," Kelsey said.

"Can you?" Tyler asked, kissing her bare shoulder.

"I can," Kelsey confirmed. Tyler released Kelsey and stood up. He walked around to the bottom of their bed.

"What are you doing?" Kelsey asked. Tyler leaned down and kissed Kelsey's ankle.

"I'll work my way up," Tyler replied.

"Here," Tyler said, much later, handing Kelsey a terry-cloth robe.

"Thank you," Kelsey replied. She sat up in bed and put it around her shoulders. She was still breathless from Tyler's thousand kisses.

"Come," Tyler said, holding out his hand to her. Kelsey took it and allowed Tyler to help her up. She felt a little weak. Tyler adjusted the terry-cloth robe around her, and tied the belt for her.

"Tired?" he asked.

"You wear me out," Kelsey replied.

"You wanted a thousand kisses," Tyler replied, unapologetically.

"I want them again tomorrow," Kelsey replied. "Same spot."

Tyler laughed delightedly.

"Come on," he said, "Let's see the view."

Tyler held her around the waist as he guided her through the suite. Kelsey looked around in interest.

"Tyler, this is beautiful," she said. Kelsey had never been in a hotel room so exquisitely decorated. Additionally, the size of the suite rivaled the one they had stayed in when they were in New York City. It was stunning.

"I'm glad you like it. Look at the view," he said, steering her out onto the terrace. The tiles were cool under Kelsey's bare feet.

Kelsey looked at the view and was absolutely speechless.

She and Tyler were standing on an enormous terrace overlooking the most spectacular view Kelsey had ever seen. All of Rome was at their feet. Church domes rose majestically in the distance, as the city sparkled in the late summer sun.

Kelsey glanced at Tyler, but she couldn't find words to describe what she was seeing.

Tyler held her close. "The Spanish Steps are right there, downstairs," he said, pointing. And Kelsey looked down at a large group of people, all milling around on a series of steps below them.

"Wow," Kelsey said. She knew that the Spanish Steps were one of the main tourist attractions in Rome, and here they were, directly above them. "Thank you," she said softly.

"Anything for my Kelsey," Tyler replied, kissing her.

As Kelsey sat at the terrace table, looking out at the view, Tyler called downstairs to have their luggage brought up. Clearly, Jeffrey had given the management Tyler's hotel rider. They would not be interrupted during their honeymoon stay by the hotel staff. Tyler walked back out onto the terrace, holding a black plate.

"Want a cookie?" he asked.

"Thanks," Kelsey said, taking one. "Where are these from?"

"A welcome gift from the hotel," Tyler replied. "They wished us a happy honeymoon."

"That was nice," Kelsey said. "So is the fact that we're honeymooning in the hotel rider this time?"

"I don't know what's in the rider. That's Jeffrey's domain."

"Do you delegate everything?" Kelsey asked.

"I didn't delegate your kisses. I made sure those were done properly," Tyler replied coolly, biting into a cookie.

"You did a good job," Kelsey said, but she blushed scarlet as she said it. She wished that she could be as nonchalant as Tyler was about sex, but it was still quite new to her. Tyler gave her a wink.

The doorbell rang, and Tyler stood up. A moment later, he returned.

"Our luggage is here. Do you want to get dressed?"

"OK," Kelsey said, standing up and biting into her cookie. She took a final look at the gorgeous view, then walked back inside the suite.

A half-hour later, Tyler lifted Kelsey off of the bottom step of the Spanish

Steps. They had taken lots of pictures on the Steps.

"We'll walk over to the Trevi Fountain on our way to dinner," Tyler said, "But I want to take you somewhere first."

Kelsey squeezed Tyler's hand happily. She was so happy to be here with him, and although they had barely left their hotel, Kelsey had already fallen in love with Italy. The ancient streets, the beautiful buildings — it all made for an amazing experience. And she had three weeks to enjoy it with the love of her life. Kelsey felt like she had never been happier.

Tyler kissed her hand as they crossed over to the Fontana della Barcaccia. They took several photographs with Tyler's Tactec tablet with the ship-like fountain behind themselves, then the couple walked on.

"This looks like a street for Jess," Kelsey commented as they passed by several designer boutiques.

"It is. This is the Via dei Condotti, Rome's most fashionable street," Tyler replied. Kelsey looked around in interest. Jessica had her eye on a Balenciaga bag which she hadn't found in the United States, and she had sent Kelsey a photo of it. Seeing if she could find it in Rome was one of Kelsey's missions during her honeymoon.

"We're going here," Tyler said, leading Kelsey into a jewelry store. The large guard opened and closed the door for them.

"What's here?" Kelsey asked.

"Your anniversary gift," Tyler replied.

Kelsey bit her lip. Tyler had given her beautiful diamond earrings just one month ago for their anniversary.

"Are you going to do this every month?" Kelsey asked.

"I want to."

"Tyler, I don't want you spending a lot of money on me. Particularly on jewelry," she added. Because from the looks and location of their hotel room, this honeymoon was going to cost Tyler a fortune.

"Did you even read our pre-nup?" Tyler asked.

"What do you mean?" Kelsey asked.

"The clause about jewelry," Tyler said helpfully. Kelsey thought back to the prenuptial agreement she and Tyler had signed before they got married. In addition to several cash payments that were outlined in the agreement, to be disbursed at various points in the marriage, there was also a clause that stated that Kelsey would be entitled to keep any jewelry she was given during the marriage, as well as the first piece of property that they purchased as a couple.

"Are you planning on divorcing me?" Kelsey asked.

Tyler narrowed his eyes at her. "Of course not. But I want to plan ahead," he said.

Kelsey frowned. "I told you. If you die, I'll kill you," she said.

"I'll keep that in mind. Pick something out."

"I don't want anything."

"Pick something out anyway," Tyler replied.

Kelsey sighed. She turned where the salespeople were patiently waiting, probably wondering why the foreign tourists were standing and talking at the door.

"I'll look," she said.

"If you don't see anything here, Cartier has a store down the street," Tyler commented. Cartier was Ryan and Jessica's favorite jeweler, and Kelsey had several pieces in her jewelry box. From Tyler's tone, Kelsey knew he was serious.

She slowly walked around the elegant store, glancing into the glass cases, while Tyler spoke to a salesman behind one of the jewelry cases. Kelsey looked at the stunning pieces, but in the back of her mind, she was wondering how to get out of receiving a gift from Tyler tonight. They had weeks to be there, and there would probably be plenty of shopping opportunities that Tyler would try to take advantage of.

"I don't see anything," Kelsey said, walking over to Tyler. The salesman had pulled something out of the case and placed it on a velvet tray.

"I found something for you," Tyler replied. Kelsey looked at him, then down at the necklace in front of Tyler.

It was incredible. A dozen stylized flowers cascaded off a chain studded with diamonds. Each flower was created out of diamonds set in gold. Kelsey was sure that she had never seen such a beautiful piece of jewelry, even including the piece that she had bought for Morgan.

"Try it on," Tyler said to her. Kelsey looked at him, then at the necklace. Gold and diamonds glistened in the light, beckoning her.

Kelsey thought she would make one last attempt, despite the fact that the salesman was picking up the necklace for Kelsey to try, and Tyler was gently lifting her hair so the chain would not get caught in it.

"Tyler, where will I wear this?" Kelsey asked, as the salesman's white-gloved hands placed the necklace around her neck.

"Jeffrey and Becks have plans for us the second we return to Seattle. You'll have plenty of chances," Tyler pointed out as he released Kelsey's hair. "Look in the mirror. It's beautiful."

Kelsey looked. He was right, it was gorgeous. The flowers glittered against her skin.

"I want you to have something memorable from the trip," Tyler continued.

"Tyler, the trip is the memory," Kelsey said helplessly. Tyler was already taking out his wallet. "Tyler, it's too much," she said. Although she had no idea how much the necklace cost, she knew from the number and size of the diamonds that it had to be a lot.

"It's the cost of a couple of nights at the hotel," Tyler said dismissively, as he handed the salesman a credit card.

Kelsey lifted an eyebrow. "What?" she said.

Tyler gave her a guilty grin.

"How much is this necklace?" she demanded.

"Twelve thousand Euros," the salesman said, handing Tyler the bill and a pen. Tyler signed it swiftly as Kelsey tried to convert Euros into dollars in her head. As she did, Tyler swept Kelsey's hair up again, and the salesman removed the necklace to package it.

"You paid over fourteen thousand dollars for that necklace?" Kelsey said as the salesman stepped away.

Tyler looked at her innocently with his big brown eyes.

"You're paying seven thousand dollars a night for our hotel?" Kelsey demanded.

Tyler looked away from her and put his card in his wallet.

"Tyler!" Kelsey whispered.

"Yes," Tyler answered.

Kelsey sighed deeply.

"Kelsey. We're on vacation. You aren't allowed to complain about costs when we're on vacation," Tyler pointed out.

The salesman returned with a black bag with the name of the store and handed it to Tyler.

"*Grazie mille,*" the salesman said.

"*Prego,*" Tyler replied, and taking Kelsey's hand, they left the store.

"Are you going to pout?" Tyler asked her as they walked down the street.

"No," Kelsey said. "Thank you. It's beautiful."

"Really? You're just going to let it go? I can buy you things?" he asked, disbelievingly.

"Yes," Kelsey said, and she meant it. "I promised you."

Tyler beamed.

"But," Kelsey said. "Please remember that I'm still trying to get used to this. You're always very generous, and I can't reciprocate."

"I don't want you to," Tyler replied.

"I know. But I want to, and I can't," Kelsey pointed out.

"You're my wife. This is our money."

"It isn't really and we both know that," Kelsey said. "Be patient. I'm trying."

"OK," Tyler conceded. "I know and I appreciate that." He lifted her hand and kissed it. "Thank you for accepting my gift."

"Thank you for giving it to me. I look forward to wearing it with you," Kelsey said.

Tyler smiled at her. "Did you want to walk around before we go back and drop this off?" he asked.

"Let's go shopping for Jess," Kelsey replied.

The couple strolled around the Via dei Condotti area. Kelsey found Balenciaga — and the purse that Jessica had been looking for. After about a half-hour, they decided to head back to the hotel, and on the way back, Kelsey spotted Sephora.

"I need one thing," she said.

"Take your time," Tyler replied, following her into the store.

Kelsey looked around the brightly-lit store quickly, and found what she was looking for. She hadn't had time to re-polish her toenails in the race to get ready to leave Seattle, and the pink polish that was there was chipping, so she decided that she would just take it off.

As she held the nail polish wipes in her hand, she debated buying a bottle of nail polish so she could redo her toes, but decided that since the store was so close, there was no need to make Tyler wait while she picked one out tonight. She went to the cashier and paid. Then she and Tyler returned to the hotel.

"We made it back outside," Tyler commented, as he held Kelsey's hand a few minutes later. They were heading to a little restaurant that the concierge at the hotel had recommended to them.

Kelsey giggled.

"My groom wants to see Rome. I'm trying to respect that," Kelsey commented. "We can get back in bed later."

"My bride probably wants dinner," Tyler commented.

"There's always room service. Should we go back?" Kelsey teased.

"Let me take you out," Tyler replied, squeezing her shoulders with his arm. Kelsey leaned against him as they slowly walked down the street.

"Thank you for bringing me here. It's wonderful," Kelsey said.

"I'm glad that you picked it," Tyler replied.

"You've been here before?" Kelsey asked.

"Briefly. We came to Europe when I was a teenager, but Lisa spent most of her time going from Tactec office to Tactec office, so we didn't stay long," Tyler replied.

"We can enjoy it together now," Kelsey said.

"We can, Princess," Tyler replied.

They strolled past little restaurants and chic shops, and every so often one of them would pause to look in a window, or to try to read one of the sign boards propped on the sidewalk that listed the day's specials in Italian.

"Your Italian is pretty good," Kelsey commented as they walked on after stopping at a third signboard.

"It's similar to Latin," Tyler replied. "But mostly, it's because I've eaten a lot of Italian food."

"It's more than that. You spoke to the salesman at the store," Kelsey replied.

"I guess," Tyler shrugged.

"Wow," Kelsey said as they approached a large column with a statue on top.

"The Column of the Immaculate Conception," Tyler said as they paused. "The Virgin Mary is on top."

"So beautiful," Kelsey said. "I'm glad we came out now. It's still light outside."

"Told you," Tyler said.

"Jess said I would love this," Kelsey said, stroking Tyler's hand with her own to acknowledge his comment. Kelsey looked around at the baroque architecture and beautiful churches as they walked.

Tyler held Kelsey's hand as they strolled silently through the busy streets.

"I wonder what it's like to live somewhere like this," Kelsey mused, as they turned a corner and passed an elegant little restaurant with sheer white curtains in the window.

"Would you like to live here?" Tyler asked.

"No, I like Seattle," she said.

Tyler kissed her. "Have you ever thought of living anywhere else?" he asked.

"Other than Seattle and Portland? Not really."

"Why?"

"I like being close to nature," Kelsey said. "And my family. If we had to move somewhere else, I would go," she said to reassure Tyler, "but I really like the Pacific Northwest."

"I'm glad, because I think we'll be there for a while," Tyler commented.

"You're not supposed to be thinking about work," Kelsey replied.

"I wasn't really. I was thinking about life," Tyler said. "It's nice to be here with you."

Kelsey beamed. "The feeling is mutual," she said.

They continued walking down the narrow streets, passing boutiques and little newsstands.

"Ready?" Tyler asked, once they reached an intersection.

"For what?" Kelsey asked. They took a few more steps, then she saw. "Beautiful," she enthused. They were standing next to the Trevi Fountain. They walked around to the front, where large crowds were standing, taking pictures, eating gelato, and throwing coins.

Kelsey stood with Tyler's arms around her waist, speechless at the sight. She had never seen anything like it in person. The huge stone facade, the exquisitely-carved statues, and of course, the sparkling blue water. It was all breathtaking.

"Here," Tyler said, handing her a two-Euro coin. "You're supposed to toss it with your right hand over your left shoulder."

"Thank you," Kelsey said taking the coin. She and Tyler turned with their backs to the fountain, and laughing, tossed their coins into the water.

"Do you think it's true? That we'll come back to Rome because we threw coins into the Trevi Fountain?" Kelsey asked, as Tyler pulled out his phone to take pictures.

"I have no idea. But I threw coins the last time I was here," Tyler replied. "Smile," he said, and he took a photo of Kelsey.

"Coins?" Kelsey asked.

"You throw three if you're single," Tyler replied. "The first guarantees your return to Rome, your second is for romance, and the third is for marriage."

"Oh, I see," Kelsey said. Tyler put his hands around her waist once more, and they gazed at the water. Kelsey leaned her head back on his chest. After a moment, Tyler took her hand, and they walked away from the crowds, toward another narrow street.

"We'll go back after sunset," Tyler said.

They had decided to eat an early dinner, because — despite their time in bed — they were both still jet lagged. Adapting to the Italian dinner schedule of dining at 9 at night would have to wait.

They ate at a casual little pizzeria that the concierge had recommended. Tyler had pizza, Kelsey had rigatoni al carbonara, and they shared a piece of tiramisu, because both of them wanted to get gelato on the walk back home.

After their leisurely dinner, and with gelato in hand, they returned to the Trevi Fountain. The sun had set during their meal, and the crowds around the fountain had thinned out. They enjoyed the view of the fountain once more —then, hand in hand, they walked back to the hotel.

Tyler opened the door to their suite a few minutes later and turned on the light. Kelsey looked at the elaborate wood paneling and the beautiful art that hung over the luxurious sofa.

"Tyler, does this hotel room actually cost seven thousand dollars a night?" Kelsey asked.

Tyler didn't speak for a moment, and Kelsey could tell that he was trying to find a way to get around answering the question.

"Yes." he finally said. "I didn't have that much of a choice, though. Conor said that we needed to stay in one of a dozen hotels in Rome that he felt had adequate security for us, if we didn't want him tagging along. This was one of them."

"OK, but we didn't have to stay in a suite. I'm sure the rooms are cheaper."

"I wanted you to have a nice experience. This is our honeymoon, and I wanted it to be special for you."

Kelsey wanted to protest, to tell Tyler that she would have a nice experience no matter where they stayed, but she knew that he already knew that was true. She felt like there was something else, something deeper, in the choices that Tyler had made for their trip, but she didn't want to discuss them now. Maybe not at all.

"Well, then," Kelsey said, tossing her hair back. "I guess we should make the most of this suite. Starting with the bedroom."

They lay in the bedroom a while later, with the soft sounds of tourists trickling in from the street. Tyler had left the balcony door open. A lamp gently illuminated the room, as Kelsey lay in Tyler's arms and held his hand.

"Tyler?"

"Yes, Princess?"

"Why did you buy the necklace for me?" Kelsey asked.

"It was pretty," Tyler replied.

"No, that's not why. You mentioned the pre-nup and said that you were planning ahead."

Tyler remained silent, so Kelsey continued.

"You aren't planning on divorcing me, and I've forbidden anything bad from happening to you, and I'm certainly not going anywhere, so what's wrong?"

"I always fight so hard to control the things that I can, because my world always seems to be in chaos," Tyler said. "Maybe Ryan's right. Maybe I should meditate."

"Tyler, that's not an answer," Kelsey replied. "Why are you preparing me to take care of myself financially?"

Kelsey knew that was the real reason for the gifts of jewelry from Tyler. He had said before that even after they were married, if anything happened to him, Lisa would never allow Kelsey to inherit anything beyond their pre-nuptial agreement.

"You're worrying me," Kelsey admitted. And he was. *What was Tyler keeping from her?*

Tyler stroked Kelsey's hand with his own.

"When I was little, we lived in Fremont," Tyler said, referring to the artsy Seattle neighborhood where he and Kelsey had gone on many dates. "We lived in a one-bedroom apartment and Chris had a shared studio a few blocks away."

Kelsey snuggled deeper into Tyler's arms. He rarely spoke about his childhood, and she was curious about what he was about to tell her.

"At some point, I don't remember when, Chris left the apartment and started sleeping at the studio. It wasn't a big deal to me though, because every morning Mom and I would have breakfast together, then she would walk me over to the studio before she went to work on Tactec. She worked in Bellevue, and we didn't have a car, so work was a long commute for her."

Kelsey was amazed that Tyler remembered all of this, because he had been so young when his parents divorced. She realized, though, that maybe his parents had filled in some of the details over time. Or perhaps — and the thought saddened her — the events were so traumatic that he still remembered them.

"Chris would keep an eye on me during the day. We'd listen to the radio as he worked, and he would feed me lunch, and sometimes dinner, because Mom was often late."

"One night, I said goodbye to Chris, and Mom walked us home. When we got there, Keiko and Zach were sitting outside of our apartment in their car. Mom told me that I would spend the night with Zach. I didn't mind, because Zach had a lot of toys. So I got in the car with them, and we left.

"When Mom showed up at the Payne house, I thought we were going back to Seattle, but Mom said, no, that we were going to stay with Bob and Ryan. I didn't know Ryan that well, but I thought it would be OK because Ryan had a lot of toys too. The thing Ryan didn't have any more was a mom, because when we got there, Cherie had already left.

"We spent the weekend with them, and on Monday, Mom was heading back to work. Before she left, I asked if we were going home. And Lisa said, no, we were going to stay with Bob and Ryan for a while, so she could be closer to work. So I asked about whether Chris was coming to live with us, and she said that he would stay in Seattle, at the studio.

"I asked Lisa if I was going to the studio while she was at work, and Lisa said no, I would stay with Ryan and Mrs. Bridges, his nanny, and that it would be fun. So she left for work. And I didn't see Chris again for seven years."

Kelsey felt her heart break at those words. She had known that Tyler and Chris had been apart for a long time, but the tone of Tyler's voice as he said it — flat, as if to dull the pain — made the truth seem more real.

Tyler continued.

"We stayed with Bob and Ryan for six months. I guess it was part of Lisa's plan to prove to the divorce court that we were poor. And whenever I asked about Chris, Lisa said he was working. Eventually I knew it was a lie, though, because even when Chris was working, he always had time for me."

Kelsey felt tears come to her eyes, and Tyler gently brushed them away.

"This is my sad story, not yours," he teased. Kelsey wiped her eyes with the back of her hand, and Tyler gave her a kiss.

"I learned a lot of lessons from losing Chris," Tyler said thoughtfully, "So when I met you, I tried so hard not to fall in love with you, because I knew I couldn't bear to lose you. Ryan and Zach spent months trying to convince me that this was different, that I could let my guard down, and that I could be happy with you. But they were wrong, and I was right, because you were ripped away from me too."

Kelsey could hear the bitterness in Tyler's voice.

"And when I watched you leave with Jessica, I promised myself that I would never assume that anyone I loved would be in my life forever." Tyler looked at Kelsey and brushed a strand of hair away from her face.

"I won't let my guard down again," he said fiercely. "I will protect you. Lisa may have my money wrapped up in trusts, but I will make sure that you never want for anything, even if I have to give you diamonds every day."

Kelsey felt the tears stream down her face, but she let them fall. She felt so many emotions from Tyler at once. The heartbreak that Tyler had suffered at such a young age. The helplessness that he had faced. The anger that he felt now.

"I'm so sorry," Kelsey said, stroking his face. "I'm so sorry that happened to you."

"I didn't mean to make you cry," Tyler said, wiping more of her tears away.

"Thank you for telling me. I understand now," Kelsey said. Everything made sense to her. This was why Tyler spoiled her, and made sure that she wanted for nothing. He made sure that every moment was special, out of fear that the moments would not last.

Kelsey leaned her head on his chest and cried.

The next morning Kelsey woke up, wrapped in Tyler's arms. She had cried herself to sleep, and Tyler had let her, knowing that her tears were out of sadness for him, and not for herself. She looked at her husband, and saw that Tyler was awake. His brown eyes were fixed on the ornate ceiling above the bed, and he was clearly thinking.

"Good morning," Kelsey said, and Tyler turned to her.

"Princess," Tyler said, kissing her. "Are you OK?"

Kelsey nodded. She didn't want to cry again, and she had no idea what to say to Tyler. Her childhood, her mistakes — she had caused them all herself. She hadn't had to pay the price for her parents' actions. Tyler had paid a high price for his.

"I don't want you to feel sorry for me," Tyler said briskly.

"I know."

"A lot of good has come with the bad," Tyler continued. "I've moved on."

"Have you? Because I don't think you have," Kelsey replied. "You're still reacting to your losses." She knew that she sounded a little harsh, but she didn't want Tyler hiding from his feelings.

"That's true," Tyler conceded. "But it's like when you burn your hand on the stove. You're always a little more careful when you're cooking. You don't want it to happen again, but there's only so much you can do to stop it."

"I see," Kelsey said. She understood what Tyler was saying. He knew that he couldn't guarantee that they wouldn't be separated again. No one could, because life wasn't assured. However, he could do what he could to make her life better if they were separated. And clearly he intended to.

"Do you ever think that you ever will move on? That you'll accept that we're always going to be together?" she asked.

Tyler was thoughtful for a moment before he spoke. "No," he finally said. "I will never take my happiness for granted."

Kelsey stroked his chest with her hand. She felt so sad. Two months into their marriage, Kelsey felt calm and hopeful about them building a life together. Tyler was on the path with her, but he would forever have an eye out for anything that threatened his love. She knew that he would never feel the certainty she felt, the feeling that nothing would get in the way of their being together. He would never be able to enjoy the bliss that came with being naive. Tyler knew too much about loss, and therefore would always protect his heart.

Kelsey now understood something that she had always wondered about. Tyler had waited, and waited, and waited even more before asking her on a date. It had been so frustrating for her and she had never fully understood why. Now she did. Loss wasn't something that Tyler dealt with as it occurred. It was burned into his soul. Kelsey felt that if she had lived Tyler's life, she never would have been willing to love again.

But here they were.

"I'm proud of you," Kelsey said, and Tyler looked at her questioningly.

"Why?" he asked.

"Because you took the risk to be with me," Kelsey said.

"There's nowhere else I'd rather be," Tyler replied.

Tyler ordered room service, and they ate breakfast on the terrace, the beauty of Rome at their side. Kelsey placed her linen napkin down on the marble table and picked up her toast. She took a bite and chewed it thoughtfully. She reached her foot out and stroked Tyler's leg with her toes. He smiled at her.

"You know that you've already given me enough money to live on for the rest of my life. I don't need anything else."

"Don't be silly. No one could live on what I've given you," Tyler replied.

Kelsey raised her eyebrows. Between Tyler and Lisa, Kelsey now owned almost five million dollars' worth of real estate in Port Townsend, plus she had five million in cash, which Papa Jefferson was busily investing in stocks for her. Kelsey would never need to work again.

"Normal people could," Kelsey replied. "And I'm pretty normal."

"Kels, I couldn't live on my salary from Simon," Tyler pointed out.

"You couldn't, I can," Kelsey replied. "Anyway, the building in PT generates twice what I make at Simon's. I don't need anything else."

"Life is expensive, Kelsey," Tyler protested.

"Your life is, because you don't know how to be poor," Kelsey said with a grin.

"What about your security? Travel? Those things cost money."

"Again, those things cost you a lot of money. The average person doesn't need a security guard, or to stay in a deluxe hotel."

"Do you think that you're still average?" Tyler asked.

Kelsey took a bite of her toast and considered the question.

"I think Mrs. Tyler Olsen isn't," she admitted. "But our hypothetical imagines a time when you aren't with me, which of course, isn't going to happen."

Tyler contemplated Kelsey's words.

"You're fearless, aren't you?" he said.

"I don't have a reason to be afraid," Kelsey replied. "I love that you take care of me. But I don't need anything else but you."

Tyler reached out and took Kelsey's hand. He kissed her fingertips.

"I have a lot to learn about you, don't I?"

"I hope so," Kelsey replied.

Around noon, Kelsey and Tyler walked out of the hotel lobby. The doorman gave them a quick bow as he held the door open for them.

They walked through the plaza and down the Spanish Steps, then Tyler led them back past the Fontana della Barcaccia, where tourists were taking photos of themselves next to the ship. Kelsey glanced at Sephora as they passed by and realized that she hadn't taken off her toenail polish. She would remember tonight, as she would be wearing open-toed shoes. In every one of the three cities they planned to visit, Tyler planned to take her for a formal dinner, and tonight was one of those nights.

They strolled down the street in the September sun. Narrow Roman streets suddenly turned into wide piazzas holding chic outdoor cafes and luxury stores.

Kelsey and Tyler walked slowly, savoring every moment. Despite their coins in the Trevi Fountain, who knew when they would be in Rome again after this trip?

Kelsey felt the gentle warmth of Tyler's hand as they headed down the Via del Corso. She always learned things about Tyler when they spent time alone together, and being in Rome was no different. A part of her was surprised that she hadn't heard the story of the last time Tyler had seen Chris as a small child. But then again, part of her wasn't.

Both she and Tyler seemed quite happy to ignore their pasts, and to talk only of the future. But Kelsey knew that despite this, both of them had been shaped in profound ways by their pasts. She suspected that Tyler knew this as well.

Kelsey never wanted to talk about her teenage years. Invariably, she looked on them with shame and embarrassment. Despite this, Kelsey knew that having been through that experience had fundamentally changed her. She wouldn't be the Kelsey she was today if she hadn't been the 13-year-old Kelsey. Her experiences on the wrong side of the justice system had led her to become a lawyer. The focus she took to work every day was developed because of the drive she had to attempt to redeem herself.

And she knew how precious it was to wake up in the morning, because if the tree she had driven into had fallen just a few more inches over, Kelsey would not have woken up with a broken leg — she would not have woken up at all. She would have lost her life.

Kelsey's teenage years would always be a cautionary tale for her, a guidepost for her to remember how easy it was to go too far in the quest for immediate gratification.

But it was a cautionary tale that she didn't like to share. Not even with Tyler.

They had wordlessly made a deal, Kelsey and Tyler had. They would share the barest outlines of their pasts, and in exchange, the other person would accept the information without judgement, but also without requesting more. Kelsey never asked deep questions about Tyler's childhood, and he never asked about hers. They would share about their pasts, or not, when they chose to.

Now, though, Kelsey was feeling strange about their unspoken deal. Tyler had shared his past to her, and because of it, Kelsey was feeling as if she was keeping secrets. She was fascinated by Tyler's past, because like her, she knew that it had made him the Tyler she loved. But she didn't feel like she could ask for more. Because then she would have to share. And Kelsey wasn't sure that she was ready to do that.

Not even with Tyler.

They stopped at the Marcus Aurelius Column, which had intricately-carved battle scenes all the way up the marble tower. Tyler stood at the base, and looked up with his big brown eyes.

"It's incredible," Kelsey said, looking up with him.

"History in the middle of the city," Tyler said, looking down at the Latin inscription.

"What does it say?" Kelsey asked.

"That the statute was restored by pope Sixtus V," Tyler replied.

"That's it?" Kelsey asked him.

"I guess the column speaks for itself, Kels," Tyler said with a smile.

"True," Kelsey said, looking back up at the column. The attention to detail was stunning. She turned to Tyler, and he retook her hand. They walked on.

"Around every corner is something else to see. I love that," Kelsey said happily.

"Seattle is too young to have so much history just scattered around," Tyler commented.

"What's next?" Kelsey asked.

"I guess we'll have to see," Tyler replied with a wink.

A few minutes later, they walked into the Palazzo Sciarra Colonna Carbognano. The 17th-century mansion was covered with art and beautifully-painted ceilings. A sun-filled atrium was the highlight for the couple.

They continued through Piazza Venezia, and turned on the Via dei Fori Imperiali. They paused to look at the Forum of Caesar, but did not stop, as they had tickets to go the next evening. They walked, pausing at statues and sneaking kisses, but they were mostly quiet, enjoying being together, surrounded by history.

"Oh, wow!" Kelsey said excitedly just a few minutes later. They had reached the Colosseum.

As a surprise for Kelsey, Jeffrey had arranged for a private tour guide to meet the couple and take them on a tour of the Colosseum and the Roman Forum. For three hours, Tyler and Kelsey walked through ancient sites and learned about Roman history. Tyler took lots of pictures, while both he and Kelsey peppered their guide with questions.

After the tour, Kelsey leaned on Tyler's shoulder as they drove back to the hotel in a private car that had been arranged for them.

"Tired, Princess?" Tyler asked, kissing her.

"A little," Kelsey admitted. "I think I'm still jet-lagged."

"We can take a break. Our dinner reservation isn't until 8:30."

"That's fine. I'll wake up by then," Kelsey said, cuddling against him.

Back at the hotel, and a short nap later, Kelsey sat on the edge of the rose marble bathtub with the bathroom door open. She had her nail polish wipes in hand, and was balancing one leg on the other in able to reach her toes.

"Are you OK?" Tyler asked, stopping at the door.

"I'm fine. I'm taking off my toenail polish," she replied.

"You don't look comfortable. Let me help you," Tyler said, walking into the bathroom. He knelt at her feet, and she handed him a sealed wipe.

"Thank you," she said. "Are you trying to butter me up so I'll sleep with you?" she teased.

Tyler laughed. "Somehow, I don't think I'll have any trouble getting you to go to bed with me, Princess." he replied. He glanced at the packet in his hand and tore it open. Then he coughed.

"What's in this?" he asked, flipping over the packet. "Acetone? You put that on your skin?" he asked her in concern.

"That's how you take the nail polish off, Tyler," Kelsey said.

Tyler frowned. "Interesting," he said, as he took the pad and wiped the nail polish off Kelsey's toes.

A half-hour later, Kelsey was ready. She walked into the living room where Tyler sat, dressed in a navy-blue suit and sending a message on his phone.

"I'm ready," Kelsey said. Tyler looked up and beamed at her. She smiled back.

"You're wearing your new necklace," Tyler commented as he stood and placed his phone into his pants pocket. Kelsey nodded. Her stomach was doing little flips. Tyler looked amazing in a suit.

"Let's go," Tyler said, taking Kelsey's hand.

"Wait, I should get my purse," Kelsey said.

"We're staying here, you don't need it," Tyler replied.

"We're eating in the hotel?" Kelsey asked in surprise. "I thought we were going somewhere special."

"The restaurant has a Michelin star," Tyler said. "Is that special enough?"

"I stand corrected," Kelsey said in awe.

In fact, the restaurant was only a few steps away from their sixth-floor suite. After Tyler pulled out her chair for her and she sat down, Kelsey looked around the lavish dining area, and out at the stunning view from the restaurant, much like the one from her room.

"You look beautiful," Tyler said.

"Thank you," Kelsey replied. She felt beautiful. Her blonde hair was in a long braid — so as not to distract from the beauty of her necklace — the diamond earrings that Tyler had given her for their first-month anniversary sparkled in her ears, and she was wearing a simple, but very elegant cream-colored silk dress, along with satin Jimmy Choo heels.

"You always look beautiful," Tyler said.

"Thank you," Kelsey repeated, with a smile.

Tyler ordered the tasting menu for them, and as the waiter took their menus away, Tyler took Kelsey's hands into his own.

"I wanted to talk to you," he said, gently touching Kelsey's wedding ring with his thumb. "About last night."

Kelsey looked at Tyler in surprise. She wasn't expecting Tyler to bring his past up again. She certainly wouldn't have.

"I want you to know that you can always ask me anything," he said thoughtfully. "I got the sense that you were hesitant to ask me questions. But I don't want you to feel bad about talking to me about anything. I've dealt — am dealing with — my childhood. It's a part of who I am, and I don't mind you wanting to know things about me."

Kelsey looked at Tyler in surprise. He had said the exact opposite of what she had expected him to.

Tyler continued. "I know that it might feel strange to ask me questions about something you've probably read about in the media. But you're my wife, so you can know whatever you want to."

Kelsey thought about Tyler's words. Of course, that might be why he would assume that she hadn't asked questions. Lisa and Chris's bitter divorce was practically a part of the Tactec story.

"I feel strange because I don't want to talk about my childhood," Kelsey blurted out. She bit her lip and cursed her honesty.

"That's fine. It's not a quid pro quo," Tyler said. "Anyway, I bet Jace has told me most of the good parts," he said with a grin.

Kelsey's mouth dropped open. "That's not funny, Tyler," she said, pulling her hands from his.

Tyler pondered her for a moment. "OK, I'm sorry," he said, gently taking her hands back.

"What did he tell you?" Kelsey demanded.

"A lot," Tyler replied.

"Before or after our wedding?" Kelsey asked, knowing the answer.

"Before. He said I should know what I was getting into," Tyler replied.

Kelsey sighed.

"Kelsey, I told you. You haven't done anything that Ryan hasn't done six times over. I don't care."

"I know. I feel bad about it, though."

"Why? You were a kid."

"I caused a lot of problems, Tyler."

"I'm sure you've made up for them. Anyway, you've heard plenty of stories about what a brat I was."

"You were practically a baby. It's completely different."

Tyler shook his head. "You haven't heard the stories of the teenage years," he said.

In fact, Kelsey had heard one of them. When Tyler had been sent into treatment for his eating disorder the first time, he had destroyed his room and been thrown out. But Tyler hadn't told her the story. Zach had.

"Will you tell me some?" Kelsey asked.

"If you'd like," Tyler replied.

Kelsey shook her head no. "I'd rather pretend you're the angel that you are now," she said.

Tyler laughed. "I'm no angel," he commented.

"You are to me," Kelsey said with a smile.

Tyler lifted her hand and kissed it. "So what do you want to know?" Tyler asked.

Kelsey surveyed his eyes. He looked completely serious. "Nothing right now," she said breezily. "Let's just have dinner."

"Kelsey," Tyler said quietly.

She looked at his questioning eyes. "What?" she said.

"Ask me," he pressed.

Kelsey sighed deeply. She did have a question, and it was very personal. She decided to ask anyway.

"How do you know that Bob and Lisa weren't having an affair?"

Tyler looked at Kelsey curiously.

"That's an interesting question. I didn't expect that one. Wow." He was quiet for a moment, then asked, "Do you think they were?"

"I guess I was wondering why the two of you moved in with Bob, and not with the Paynes. Lisa and Keiko have been friends since college, but your mom had only met Bob a couple of years earlier."

"Good point. I think that since both of their spouses had left them with children, they thought they could help each other. That's why they moved next door to each other. Or at least that's what they say," he added.

"You don't think that they were having an affair?" Kelsey said. From Tyler's demeanor, it was clear that he didn't.

"I can't say with certainty that they didn't. But Lisa and Bob are very different people. They get along tremendously well, and have managed to build a business together, but I think they know that they would not be able to build a home together."

Kelsey considered Tyler's words. She supposed he had a point. Lisa Olsen was very serious and deliberate in life, and from having met three of the men that Lisa had dated, Kelsey knew that they were quite serious too. Creating a long-term relationship with the fun-loving Bob Perkins probably had never crossed Lisa's mind.

"That's true," Kelsey agreed.

"Also I think Lisa would kill him if she was dating him," Tyler said.

Kelsey burst out laughing. "I think so too," she agreed.

"That's it? All you want to know about me is why Bob Perkins isn't my stepfather?" Tyler asked.

"Maybe for now," Kelsey said. She looked into his chocolate-brown eyes. "Actually, it breaks my heart thinking about you as a child."

"Why?"

"I know how hard it was for me when my parents weren't getting along. I can't imagine how it must feel when they never get along."

"You get used to it," Tyler replied.

"Do you?"

"You have to, Kels. There's nothing you can do about it."

"I guess. I would probably try to force them to get along."

"Lisa and Chris?"

"OK, maybe not," Kelsey agreed.

"Exactly," Tyler said. Kelsey looked up. The waiter seemed to be contemplating them from a distance.

"Maybe he doesn't want to interrupt our conversation," Tyler commented.

"Maybe," Kelsey said. Tyler kissed her hands, and let go of them. "We have seven courses. If he doesn't start, we'll be here all night."

"At least our room is close by," Kelsey reminded him.

Hours later, Kelsey found herself pressed against the front door of their suite, kissing Tyler. His hands were feverishly looking for the zipper on Kelsey's dress, but she was too busy kissing him to tell him how to find it. The dinner that had begun on a serious note, had segued into romantic, and turned passionate. And Kelsey was loving every second of it.

Tyler's hands found the zipper, and he pulled it down with a sharp yank. Luckily the dress didn't rip, but instead it fell to the ground as Tyler pushed it off Kelsey's shoulders.

"You're wearing red," Tyler said huskily.

"For you," Kelsey said, pulling him towards herself. His tie was already on the floor, as was his jacket, and she had unbuttoned most of the buttons on his shirt. Tyler slipped his hands around her back and stroked her neck. The necklace clasp rubbed against Kelsey, but she paid it no mind. Tyler's hands undid her bra strap and Kelsey felt the bra loosen.

"You're getting good at that," she whispered.

"Practice makes perfect," Tyler replied, leaning down and kissing her bare collarbone. Kelsey sighed with delight.

Tyler slipped his thumb underneath the left bra strap and tugged it forward. The strap slipped down Kelsey's arm, and took the bra with it.

"That's better," Tyler said, kissing her chest again.

"You're too far ahead," Kelsey complained. In her hot and bothered state, she was having trouble with Tyler's buttons.

"Sorry," Tyler said, undoing the buttons on his shirt, "I'll help."

"Thanks," Kelsey said, reaching down to undo the button on his pants.

"No. Thank you," Tyler said, kissing her neck. Kelsey giggled, and Tyler's pants fell to the floor. A moment later, his white shirt followed.

Kelsey stroked Tyler's bare chest with her hands as he kissed her deeply. Suddenly, he swept her up into his arms and she clung to his neck, hanging on breathlessly. And without a word, he carried her into the bedroom.

"How did we get here?" Kelsey asked Tyler a while later. The cool tiles under her back contrasted with her warm body and fast breathing.

"You don't remember?" Tyler asked, kissing her. He was hot as well.

"I don't remember anything."

"I could remind you."

"OK, I remember that," Kelsey giggled, cuddling against Tyler. Like her, he was also lying on the bathroom floor. Kelsey could barely think straight, but she was very, very happy. She ran her hand down Tyler's bare arm, and closed her eyes.

"Do you want to take a bath?" Tyler asked.

Kelsey opened her eyes. "Seriously?"

"Sure," Tyler said, kissing Kelsey and standing up. "I need to cool off." He walked to the bathtub and turned on the water.

Kelsey sat up. "We could take a shower," Kelsey said.

"I need to cover your beautiful body up with bubbles if you ever want to go to bed," Tyler replied. He took a small bottle of soap off the counter, opened it and poured some of it into the bathtub. Kelsey watched him as he gathered two towels and placed them on the bath stool. Then he shut the water off.

"Are you coming in?" he asked.

"Yes," Kelsey said, and Tyler reached down and pulled her up. He held her waist as she stepped into the deliciously cool water, then he held her hands as she sat down. The water was the perfect temperature. Kelsey moved her legs to the side as Tyler entered the water, facing her.

"Here," he said, arranging her legs so they were balanced on his own. Kelsey wiggled her toes at him.

Tyler took her foot into his hand and stroked it.

"I need to polish my nails," Kelsey said, as Tyler began to rub her foot.

"Wait until later. Does that feel good?" he asked.

"Very," Kelsey said. "I didn't realize that I would get a foot massage too."

"I provide full service," Tyler said. Kelsey laughed, and rubbed the back of her neck.

"Oh!" she said in surprise. "I'm still wearing my necklace."

"Here, I'll take it," Tyler said. Kelsey reached around and removed the necklace. She handed it to Tyler, who placed it gently on the towels.

"Thanks," Kelsey said. She sat back in the bubbles, and the cool water brushed her shoulders. "That feels great, Tyler," she said. Tyler had resumed her foot massage.

"We definitely need to have a bathtub big enough for two," Tyler said.

"I'd say tell Jeffrey, but he's here," Kelsey said.

"Camille is in charge of renovating our new house," Tyler said. "I'll message her later."

"Do you think they'll be done by the time we get back?" Kelsey asked. The condo in Seattle was quite large, and there had been some doubt whether they would move into it, or back into the Belltown condo, when they returned from Italy.

"If Camille wants them to be, they will," Tyler replied. Kelsey smiled. She didn't know Camille, but she seemed like a take-charge kind of person. Kelsey supposed that as Lisa's longtime assistant, that would be a job requirement. "I told her it didn't matter if they needed an extra couple of weeks. I'd prefer that they get it done right."

"Me too," Kelsey said blissfully. Tyler had switched feet when he was talking, and her right foot felt very relaxed and cozy.

"Did you have any special requests?" Tyler asked.

"I just asked Jeffrey to make sure there was a treadmill somewhere," Kelsey said. She said it nonchalantly, but actually she had very mixed feelings about their move. Although she knew that it didn't matter to Tyler, her desire to be closer to work was going to require him to spend money on renovating a very large space. At least he had already owned it, and they could rent out the Belltown condo. Those facts made her feel better.

"You're easy to please," Tyler said, as he kneaded away the tension in Kelsey's sole.

"I'm making you move across downtown. I'm not that easy to please," Kelsey replied.

"I'll be closer to work too," Tyler said. "Maybe I won't buy a car after all."

"I thought you wanted a Tesla," Kelsey said. Tyler had been renting a car ever since Lisa told him to get rid of the Porsche after the Tactec picnic.

"I do. And I can almost afford one."

Kelsey smiled. "That sounds really weird," she said.

"I'm a married man now. I have to save up for things," Tyler teased.

"I might be able to afford a Tesla on my salary," Kelsey said. "Should I buy you one?" she teased.

"No. Save your money," Tyler said firmly.

"For our non-existent separation," Kelsey said.

"So you can start your own company a few years after you make partner," Tyler said. "I thought you wanted to earn the money yourself."

"I do. Maybe I shouldn't be trying to become partner if I want to follow in Lisa Olsen's footsteps. She never made partner."

"I put an end to that dream for her," Tyler said. Lisa had been put on the mommy track at her law firm when she had been pregnant with Tyler, and knew she would never make partner.

"Good job. That's why she started Tactec. Like you said, partners don't become billionaires. Another reason for me to rethink being partner."

"You have some time. Although I bet Bill would make you partner."

"I don't think there are going to ever be partners at Simon and Associates," Kelsey said.

"You never know. Bill likes you."

"Maybe," Kelsey said. Tyler set her left foot down, and reached for her right one again. "It's OK. Thank you," she said.

"Your feet feel good?"

"Perfect," Kelsey said. "Do you want a foot massage?"

Tyler shook his head no. "I'm good. Thanks," he said. Kelsey closed her eyes. "Do you want to go to bed?"

"We probably should. I'm completely relaxed now."

"I'm glad. I want you to have fun on this trip," Tyler said.

Kelsey opened her eyes at his tone. "Why are you so stressed out about my having fun?" she asked.

"It's going to be a while before our next vacation," Tyler replied.

"Not really. Thanksgiving is coming up," Kelsey said, closing her eyes again.

"You never seem to find Port Townsend relaxing," Tyler replied.

Kelsey's eyes flew open. "We're going to Port Townsend for Thanksgiving?" she asked.

"Of course we are," Tyler replied.

"Says who?"

"Says your father," Tyler said "He wants to check on you. I thought you knew that."

"I must have blocked it out," Kelsey said.

"Anyway," Tyler continued, "if we're going to Lisa's for Christmas, I certainly don't want to spend Thanksgiving there too."

"I suppose," Kelsey said. She and Tyler had very briefly discussed alternating holidays with their respective parents ages ago. She had just forgotten.

"It will be strange not having Morgan there," Tyler said, as he stood up in the bath. "Where will I stay when your mother throws me out?"

"We're staying at my new house. No way are we staying at my parents," Kelsey said.

"That should work then," Tyler said. He moved Kelsey's necklace to the counter and picked up a towel. He began to dry himself off.

"Grandma's probably going to move in too," Kelsey said thoughtfully.

"It's just a weekend," Tyler said. "Can I help you up?" he asked.

"Thanks," Kelsey said, reaching out to him with her arms. Tyler gently pulled her out of the water.

"Can I dry you off?" Tyler asked seductively. Kelsey took the other towel off the bath stool.

"No," she said firmly. "I want to go to bed."

"That's what I had in mind," Tyler replied.

Kelsey frowned and he laughed. He pulled her into his arms and kissed her deeply. They stood in the bathroom, separated only by the soft white towel still in Kelsey's hands. Kelsey looked up at Tyler's sexy brown eyes. Then she stood on her tiptoes and kissed his nose.

"Goodnight, Mr. Olsen," she said.

"It will be," Tyler replied. "Because you're with me."

The sun shone onto Kelsey's bare back as she lay in Tyler's arms the next morning. He kissed her shoulder.

"That was a nice way to wake up," he said.

Kelsey looked into Tyler's sexy eyes, and stroked his face.

"I like waking up next to you," she said softly. Tyler nuzzled her, and Kelsey closed her eyes contentedly. But there was a question on her mind.

"Why do you love me?" she asked, opening her eyes once more.

Tyler looked thoughtful as Kelsey lay on his arm. He stroked her hair. Kelsey smiled as she waited for his answer. Kelsey knew that her question would not be answered with a nervous joke, or brushed aside. She knew that Tyler would treat her question seriously, with respect. It was one of the many things that she loved about him.

"There's a lot of reasons," Tyler said. "You're really smart, and of course, you're beautiful. But I think one of the things that most attracted me to you is that you're non-judgmental. I can tell you anything and you won't spend time trying to convince me that I'm wrong for feeling the way that I do."

"Really?" Kelsey said. "But I don't always agree with you."

"I know, but even when you don't agree with me, I know that I'll get your well-reasoned opinion why you don't. You don't spend a lot of energy trying to pull me over to your way of thinking."

"Is that good?" Kelsey asked.

"I think it's helpful. I look forward to talking to you when things are bothering me, because I know you'll listen. You are concerned about me, and my feelings, first."

"Why wouldn't I be?" Kelsey asked. She was a little confused, and Tyler smiled at her look.

"Because in my experience, the only person whose feelings matter are Ms. Lisa Olsen's. Because she makes the money."

Kelsey considered Tyler's words. She supposed that was true. In fact, she had seen it herself.

"Everyone falls over themselves to make sure that Lisa is happy. And that would be fine, if so many of my desires didn't conflict with her goals. So it's nice to have someone who thinks about what I want, and is on my side."

Tyler surveyed Kelsey. "Do you know what I mean?"

"Not really," she admitted.

"One of the reasons that I never brought anyone home for Lisa to meet," Tyler said, and Kelsey knew that he was talking about past girlfriends, "is because I knew that they would be focused on making a good impression on Lisa. I would be an afterthought."

"Everyone wants to make a good first impression," Kelsey said.

"I'm not sure I'm explaining this well," Tyler thought. "OK," he said, and Kelsey snuggled deeper into his arms. She was quite cozy. "At the holiday party. Did you expect to meet Lisa?"

Kelsey thought back to when Tyler had invited her to her first Tactec party.

"No, I was there because you asked me to be," she said.

"If I hadn't introduced you, would you have asked me to?"

"No," Kelsey said. "It wouldn't have crossed my mind."

"That makes you different from virtually everyone else I've ever met,"

Tyler said. "You aren't interested in flattering people. You're interested in building something for yourself. Something with me. I love that about you," he continued. "A lot of people have tried to use me as a stepping stone to get to Lisa. I've met women who are interested in being Lisa Olsen's daughter-in-law, not Tyler Olsen's wife. You're my Kelsey, and that means so much to me."

"So you like me because I'm poorly behaved?" Kelsey asked.

Tyler laughed. "What do you mean?"

"I don't know, you make it sound like I'm uninterested in people," Kelsey admitted.

"I don't mean it like that. You're interested in people, but you aren't interested in what people can do for you. That's not what attracts you to someone."

Kelsey considered this. Tyler had a point.

"If I had stood in the middle of the Darrow campus, offering hundred-dollar bills to anyone who would be my friend, you are one of the few people that would have passed me by. Even if you needed the money."

Kelsey giggled. "As much as I hate to admit it, you're right," she said.

"Why do you hate to admit it? I think it's a virtue," Tyler replied.

"I guess it feels weird to think of myself like that. That I wouldn't go out of my way for a hundred bucks. I mean, how hard is it to call yourself someone's friend?"

"But that's the thing, you wouldn't just call someone your friend. You would be a friend. And you're not going to be friends with someone just because they might be able to do something for you. You have too much self-respect."

Tyler stroked her hair once more. "You're so sure, so confident about yourself, that you don't need anyone's approval to be yourself. And knowing that about you, that gives me the confidence to be myself around you. You love me for who I am, not for the money I have. You won't sugarcoat what you think, because you aren't afraid that my reaction will drive you away. You're fearless when it comes to life, and I love seeing that, because it reminds me to be fearless too. My whole life I've been told not to rock the boat, because Lisa's trying to steer, and you're here, and you say, 'Is there a boat here? Because I have some rocking to do.'"

Kelsey laughed and Tyler hugged her.

"It's funny," Kelsey said, as she stroked Tyler's bare chest. "The thing that you love most about me is the thing that bothers my mom the most. She doesn't like me to think for myself, she wants me to be well-behaved."

"I'm glad you're not, because we wouldn't be here if you were," Tyler said.

"Why?" Kelsey asked.

"You wouldn't be you, Kelsey. And," Tyler added, "I wouldn't be me."

Kelsey didn't need an explanation, because deep down she knew what Tyler meant. If she had been an ordinary girl, like the ones who flirted with Tyler at Darrow, he wouldn't have noticed her. And even if he had, if Lisa hadn't approved of her, he wouldn't have had the will to fight to marry an ordinary girl.

"You're very special, Kelsey. And that's why I love you," Tyler said, kissing her.

Kelsey was still glowing from Tyler's words as they left the hotel over an hour later. Once again, they had eaten a late breakfast on their terrace, then they had dressed for another day of walking around.

119

Tyler held Kelsey's hand gently as they walked back down the Spanish Steps, but this time the couple headed north. It was Monday, the day that most museums were closed, so they had decided that today would be a mostly free day, where they would walk, and talk and play, without trying to see the tourist sights.

They strolled through the Piazza di Spagna, and past the horse-drawn carriages that waited there. The Piazza was lined with elegant designer stores, with a guard standing at most doors, waiting to let the tourists in.

But Kelsey paid them no mind. She was enraptured by her husband, who strode next to her, holding her hand, and pausing to give her kisses.

These were her favorite moments with Tyler, and as far as they were both concerned, there were never enough of them. At moments like this, Kelsey understood why Tyler sometimes felt jealous of Ryan. Bob didn't expect Ryan to work much, and with the babies, it was possible that Ryan wouldn't set foot in a Tactec office again. Jess, if she wanted to, could remain at home with Ryan. There was no real expectation for them to contribute to the company.

Tyler, on the other hand, was the heir to the Tactec throne, and because he was working, there really wasn't a reason for Kelsey not to. Moments like this would continue to be rare for the couple.

Kelsey wondered, that if Tyler didn't have to work, would she be willing to stay home with him? Could she travel the world with him, wake up in luxury hotels with him, and just enjoy life? Kelsey had her doubts.

But it didn't matter, because Tyler Olsen was simply taking a short break with his new wife before he got on the road to become CEO of Tactec. Kelsey didn't have to delve into her own feelings, because the plan was already laid out before them. They just had to follow it.

"Are you enjoying Rome?" Tyler asked as they walked past a small outdoor restaurant.

"No, it's terrible," Kelsey teased. "I'm always out of bed because there's too much to see."

Tyler smiled at her. "So we should have had our honeymoon in Newark?" he asked.

"Maybe we should have gone back to Kalaloch," Kelsey pouted.

"We found things to do there," Tyler pointed out.

"We spent most of our time trying not to go to bed together," Kelsey reminded him. "We wouldn't have had that problem this time."

"We didn't have to have it last time," Tyler said, kissing her hand.

"Yes, we did," Kelsey said. Tyler gave her a wicked smile, and slipped his arm around her waist. Kelsey looked up at him, her low ponytail brushing against her shoulder.

"I'll try to make sure that our sightseeing doesn't get too much in the way of our honeymoon," Tyler said.

"Thank you. I'd appreciate that," Kelsey said. "Because I don't want to go back and be able to tell people that I saw Italy on my honeymoon."

Tyler laughed.

"What are you laughing at?" Kelsey asked.

"Just another thing I love about you," Tyler said, kissing her.

They walked silently, taking in the beautiful city. Every so often they would stop to take a picture of a monument, or a picture of the two of them together. Kelsey knew that Tyler shared her feelings, the knowledge that neither of them knew the next time when they would have this much free time together. They needed to make the most of it, and that meant enjoying each other's company, instead of hurrying through their day.

They stopped for late-morning gelato, and as Kelsey waited for Tyler to pay, she looked at a message from Jessica. She frowned, then nudged Tyler as he put his wallet away. Tyler looked down, and Kelsey showed him her phone. There was a photo of the two of them, taken while they had been waiting at JFK.

"I guess we were warned," Kelsey noted.

"It's fine," Tyler said. "You look beautiful."

Kelsey smiled at him. The photograph itself was actually quite nice. The photographer had taken the picture just at the moment when Kelsey was throwing her arms around Tyler's neck for a hug. They both looked very happy.

"Here," Tyler said, taking a cone from the clerk and handing it to Kelsey. Kelsey dropped her phone in her tote bag, and took the cone from his hands.

"Thanks," she said, taking a bite. It was delicious. Tyler got his own cone, and they headed out of the gelateria. They sat at one of the empty tables outside in the warm sun. Kelsey stretched out her espadrille-clad foot, and stroked Tyler's leg. He gave her a sexy smile in reply.

"Do you want to go back?" he asked.

"Soon," Kelsey replied, with the tiniest blush.

"You're so pretty when you blush," Tyler said, and Kelsey felt herself blush some more.

Tyler stroked her leg with his hand as they ate the gelato. Every time Kelsey looked up, she saw Tyler's sexy brown eyes looking right back at her, so she would look away again. But she was mesmerized by him.

She looked up just as Tyler brushed the final crumbs of his cone off his lip with his thumb, and Kelsey felt herself get very warm. Tyler noticed her look.

"Are you sure you don't want to go back?" he asked.

"Positive," Kelsey said doubtfully.

Tyler laughed, and pulled out his phone. "Think about it while you finish," he said.

Kelsey was thoughtful. In fact, she knew that she wanted to go back to the hotel room, and do nothing for the next three weeks but be in Tyler's arms. But she also loved Rome, and knew that being here was an opportunity of a lifetime. Walking around Rome with Tyler was a compromise, but a slightly unsatisfying one.

Tyler sighed deeply from across the table.

"What's up?" Kelsey asked.

"You're sure you don't mind visiting Tactec Roma on Wednesday?" he said.

"I'm sure," Kelsey said with a smile. Lisa had requested that Tyler stop by Tactec's Rome office while the couple was in Italy, and Tyler had agreed on the condition that the visit be less than 90 minutes, and that Kelsey could come along. "Work comes first," she added.

"That's Lisa's motto. I'm not sure it's mine," Tyler replied.

"I thought it was the Olsen family motto?" Kelsey asked. "I'm part of the Olsen family now."

"I think we need some new mottos," Tyler replied.

"Like what?" Kelsey asked.

"Sleep naked," Tyler replied.

Kelsey giggled. "OK, that's one for our house. What's one we can share with your mom?" she asked.

"Avoid Bill Simon?"

Kelsey shook her head no. "Not if I want to go back to work on October 1st," she said.

"I guess I'll have to think about it then. I know. Work comes last."

"But we know that's not true," Kelsey said.

"Of course you would say that," Tyler said.

Kelsey shrugged. "I have goals," she said simply.

"I do too," Tyler replied, and Kelsey saw the sparkle in his eyes. "One of them involves you and the bed in our hotel room."

Kelsey felt herself blush again, and concentrated on finishing her gelato. She took the last bite of the cone and wiped her fingers on the paper napkin, all the while avoiding Tyler's glance. Kelsey reached into her bag and pulled out her own phone to check messages.

"Look," Tyler said, holding his tablet out for Kelsey. Ryan had posted a picture of the babies with the caption *Miss you*.

"They're so sweet," Kelsey cooed. She missed them too. Kelsey looked down at her own phone. She glanced at Morgan's Instagram posts over the weekend, which featured not only the party that Morgan worked on, but also a picture of Morgan in a bikini lying in the summer sun. Kelsey knew that the photograph was for Bob, because it was unlike most of Morgan's posts.

Next, Kelsey turned to her messages. She bit her lip, and looked up at Tyler.

"I need to go back to the hotel," she said.

"He did this on purpose." Tyler groused as he and Kelsey headed back toward the hotel. Kelsey was silent, because she thought so too. Bill Simon had sent Kelsey a message requesting that she send him the draft of a document she had been working on, but that wasn't due to the client until mid-October. Because it was on her tablet, which wasn't synced to her phone, she needed to return to the hotel room to send it.

Kelsey stroked Tyler's ring with her thumb.

"It's not a big deal. It will take five minutes," Kelsey said.

Tyler glanced at her as they walked. "Does he really need it now?" he asked.

"No," Kelsey admitted.

"So he really did do this on purpose," Tyler said.

"But you started it, right?" Kelsey asked. "Last weekend?"

A smile played on Tyler's lips. "You weren't even there," he said.

"What did you do?"

"It doesn't matter. I'll take my punishment from Bill Simon. We're almost back to the hotel. Stepfathers are a pain," he added.

"Do you think they are going to get married?" Kelsey asked in surprise.

"It's only a matter of time," Tyler replied.

"What makes you say that?" Kelsey asked.

"It's just a feeling," Tyler said. "A bad one."

"Tyler, what do you really have against Bill?" Kelsey asked. "I know that you didn't like working for him, but I'm not understanding what that has to do with him dating Lisa."

"The fact that they broke up before has a little something to do with it," Tyler replied.

"That was decades ago," Kelsey replied.

"Do you think he's changed?"

"Lisa thinks so."

"Maybe she's wrong," Tyler replied. Kelsey stroked Tyler's hand again. She didn't want to fight with him, but she was curious as to his animosity towards Bill dating his mother. Kelsey didn't think that Tyler was against his mother getting remarried generally. In fact, when she had been dating her last serious boyfriend, Tyler had said that he didn't care whether Lisa got married or not. But with Bill Simon, he seemed to be actively campaigning against it.

"Do you know something that I don't?" Kelsey asked.

"It's just interesting to me that Keiko is so upset about Lisa dating him again," Tyler said.

"Well, she was there during the last break-up. Maybe she doesn't want it to happen to Lisa again," Kelsey commented.

"Maybe. I don't want to talk about Bill Simon."

Kelsey wondered whether to press Tyler on the subject, but thought the better of it. Bill Simon was likely to be in their lives for a while, either as Kelsey's boss, or as Lisa's boyfriend, or both, so Kelsey decided that the topic could wait for another day.

"That's fine," Kelsey said. "But can you avoid irritating him for a while, so I don't have to work any more during our honeymoon?"

Tyler glanced at her with his brown eyes, and gave her a smile.

"I can try," he said, kissing her hand.

"Try real hard," Kelsey said, and Tyler laughed.

They returned to their hotel room, and Kelsey sent the document over to Bill.

"You know it's two in the morning there," Tyler commented from the sofa.

"Bill messaged me at midnight Seattle time. He might still be up," Kelsey said, setting the tablet down on the table and joining Tyler on the sofa.

"Knowing him, he probably is," Tyler said. He put his arm around Kelsey and kissed her. "Help me forget about Bill Simon," he said.

"How?" Kelsey teased, kissing him back.

"LIke this," Tyler said, pulling Kelsey closer. She leaned into him, and Tyler fell back on the sofa, pulling Kelsey on top of himself. "That's better," he said, looking up at her.

"Is it?" Kelsey said softly, falling under Tyler's spell.

"It is," Tyler replied huskily, kissing Kelsey again. Suddenly Tyler's phone rang with a ringtone she hadn't heard before.

"Are you kidding me?" he said.

"Ignore it," Kelsey said.

"I can't. Hang on," Tyler said, reaching out for his phone. *"Pronto,"* he said in Italian. Kelsey shifted as if to move, but Tyler reached out and pressed her firmly against himself. She leaned back on him. This phone call wouldn't take long.

"Ciao Lorenzo, come stai?"

Tyler listened for a moment, then said, *"Sto bene."*

Another pause, then Tyler said, *"Non ti preoccupare. Va bene."*

The next pause lasted a bit longer, then Tyler ended the call with, *"OK. Ciao."* He placed the phone back on the table. "Sorry, where were we?" he asked Kelsey.

"Who was that?" she asked.

"Tactec. They want us to come at 10:30 instead of 11," Tyler said.

"When did you learn Italian?" she asked.

"I didn't. I pretty much reached the limit of my knowledge with that phone call," Tyler replied. Kelsey giggled and shifted against him. Her hair brushed his face.

"We were here," she said, kissing him.

"Maybe I should thank Bill," Tyler said two hours later. They were lying on the floor of the living room, Kelsey cuddled in his arms.

"Maybe," Kelsey agreed.

"But we aren't going to see any of Rome if we keep doing this."

"That's OK. Rome will be here when we retire," Kelsey replied.

Tyler laughed. "Is that the next time we're going to take a vacation?" he asked. "Probably," he added, answering his own question.

"We can come back when you're CEO," Kelsey said.

"You'll travel with me? When you're partner?" he asked, stroking Kelsey's hair.

"We'll see," she replied. Tyler kissed her and sighed.

"Thinking about work?" Kelsey asked.

"Thinking about life," Tyler said.

"What about it?"

"About how happy I am here. About how unhappy I'll be when I'm back in the office."

Kelsey stroked Tyler's chest with her hand.

"I should be more like you. Learn to enjoy my work," Tyler commented.

"You'll like it more when you have more control over what you are doing," Kelsey said.

"That's very insightful, Mrs. Olsen. You're probably right."

"Of course I am," Kelsey teased. Tyler held her close.

"Should we go back out?" Tyler asked.

"In a minute," Kelsey said, closing her eyes.

A while later, the couple headed out for the second time. Italian custom was to eat a late lunch, and since neither of them was particularly hungry, they decided to resume their walk.

"So I have a question for you."

"You're full of questions today, Princess," Tyler replied.

"I know. But there are things that I've always wondered about you, and I figure now is a good time to ask you," Kelsey replied.

"It's fine, I don't mind. What's the question?"

"If you could have dinner with any two people in the world, who would you choose?"

"That's the question?"

"That's it," Kelsey replied. In fact, she had been curious about Tyler's answer to this particular question. He was so scholarly, and now that they were surrounded by history, she was reminded of the fact that she wanted to ask him.

"I had it. It was with my parents," Tyler replied.

Kelsey looked at him in surprise. "That was it?" she said.

Tyler nodded. "I guess now, I'd probably pick Chris and Cherie, to figure out what they were up to," he said.

"I thought you were going to say Julius Caesar, or someone historical," Kelsey said.

"Who would you choose?"

"I think I might choose Gandhi and Nelson Mandela," Kelsey replied.

"Interesting choices. Why?"

"Both of them led revolutions against really powerful forces," Kelsey said. "I would like to understand where they got their persistence and drive in the face of so much opposition."

"Do you feel like you need that skill?" Tyler asked.

"That's an interesting question. I hadn't thought of it that way."

"I think that the purpose of the question is to draw out what someone feels is lacking in their own understanding of the world."

"Really? Then why would you want to have dinner with Chris and Cherie?"

"I'm curious as to why someone would betray people that they are committed to."

"You think of it as betrayal?"

"Yes, don't you?"

"I guess I took Chris at his word when he portrayed it as love," Kelsey replied.

Tyler shook his head. "Chris knew Cherie well before he knew Lisa, maybe even before Cherie knew Bob. But somehow Lisa got dragged into their romance."

"Maybe there wasn't a romance before Chris met Lisa," Kelsey commented.

"No? You don't think so?" Tyler said doubtfully.

"But then why would Chris marry Lisa, and Cherie marry Bob?"

Tyler shrugged.

"That's the mystery," he said. "It doesn't make sense, and that's why it feels like a betrayal. Like Chris knew something that Lisa didn't."

"Now I want to have dinner with Chris and Cherie," Kelsey said.

"Exactly," Tyler said. "But I have a feeling that even if they had dinner together, we wouldn't be invited."

Kelsey stopped to buy postcards for her parents and Grandma Rose. She paused very briefly before picking up a third postcard for her other grandparents, the Parkers. She decided to address it to her cousin instead. Despite her attempt at reconciliation with her grandparents, Kelsey had to admit that her hurt feelings were still there.

In the meantime, Tyler practiced his Italian with the clerks, who were delighted that a foreigner was willing to try to speak their language. As they left the store, Tyler offered Kelsey a piece of hard candy.

"Gift with purchase," Tyler said, opening a second one and putting it in his mouth.

They paused in one of the piazzas and Tyler took out his tablet to take a photograph. As he did so, Kelsey took out her own phone. Happily, there were no more messages from Bill Simon. She supposed that he had made his point to Tyler.

Kelsey scrolled to Instagram, where Morgan had posted an Instagram story of herself getting ready to go out. Once again, Kelsey could tell from the way Morgan had created the story, that the intended viewer was Bob. Morgan had done everything but mention him by name. Tyler walked over to Kelsey and looked over her shoulder.

"Bob and Morgan are still trolling each other?" he asked.

"Morgan certainly is," Kelsey replied.

"Tell her to post a photo of herself going out with someone else. That will get Bob's attention," Tyler commented. Kelsey looked at him curiously.

"Mr. Perkins gets quite jealous," Tyler replied.

"Bob?"

"Charlotte received significantly less money than the other ex-wives because he caught her cheating on him."

"Then won't he be upset with Morgan?"

Tyler shrugged. "They aren't married, are they? She's free to date."

Kelsey put her phone into her bag, Tyler took her hand, and they continued to walk.

"I wonder why he hasn't gotten married yet," Tyler mused.

"To Morgan?"

"To anyone," Tyler corrected. "It's been a while."

"Maybe he hasn't found anyone he likes," Kelsey said, and her heart hurt a little as she said it, because she knew how Morgan felt about Bob.

Tyler looked at Kelsey. "He likes Morgan, which is why I'm surprised he hasn't told Ryan to pound sand. But Bob likes being married too. It's weird that he's not. I just don't understand him, I guess."

"I'm not surprised that you don't understand the mindset of someone who's been married four times," Kelsey commented.

Tyler kissed the back of her hand. "I would marry you again," he said. "Every day."

Kelsey bit her lip. Usually, she would make a sarcastic remark about herself, and how Tyler didn't know the real Kelsey yet. But she refrained from doing so. As Tyler had pointed out previously, she needed to appreciate her own self, as Tyler appreciated her.

"I would marry you too. But we're married. We don't have to get married again," she replied. Tyler put his arm around her waist, and Kelsey gently leaned on him as they continued their walk.

"Is Morgan OK?" Tyler asked, returning to their previous subject.

"About Bob? I think so."

"Bob's not," Tyler said.

"He's the one who isn't interested in marrying Morgan," Kelsey pointed out.

"That's what he says. But he's not acting like it."

"What do you mean?"

"Normally, Bob doesn't play a lot of games. He's pretty decisive. But every since he started dating Morgan, it's like he can't make a decision, so she keeps getting pulled back and forth. He wants her in his life, but he won't marry her, and I really can't believe that Ryan being a jerk is the only problem."

"Maybe Bob doesn't want to get married again."

"Bob doesn't know how not to be married," Tyler said firmly.

"Why is this bothering you?" Kelsey asked.

"Because I don't like to see Morgan hurt. Because I dislike seeing Ryan being so smug. Because Bob used to be more predictable. Those are all reasons."

"I think Morgan's OK," Kelsey said, and she meant it. "I think that she's accepted that Bob's not going to marry her."

"Then what's with the Instagram posts?" Tyler asked.

Kelsey knew that Morgan had spent her entire life not getting what she wanted, and Bob Perkins was just another person in that long list. But unlike others in her past, Bob was still around, and this time Morgan had the luxury of being able to express her hurt, even if it was on the internet.

"I think that Morgan wants him to know what he's missing."

"I'm sure he does, but from the things that she's posting, it looks like Morgan's completely moved on," Tyler commented.

Kelsey thought he was right. Morgan had tried and failed to marry Bob, and despite the fact that Morgan loved him, she wasn't going to keep trying. Morgan Hill could accept defeat in a way that Kelsey had never been able to. Because throughout her life, Morgan had needed to.

Morgan had lost her mother, her stepmother, and although he was still around, she had basically lost her father as well. Morgan was a survivor, and that meant putting the bad behind her and moving forward with the good. Kelsey had grown up differently. She was a fighter, and her nature meant that she would continue to battle until all hope was lost. Kelsey mused that it was good that she had fallen in love with someone who felt the same about her.

Kelsey wasn't sure what she would do if she were in Morgan's position, but she was confident that she wouldn't be taking it as well as Morgan. Kelsey suppressed a smile as one of Eric's wry comments popped into her head. *I don't imagine too many guys would be dumb enough to break up with you,* Eric had said, and Kelsey knew that there was at least a little truth to that statement.

Unlike Morgan, Kelsey probably wouldn't have taken Bob Perkins' inability to commit well. In fact, Kelsey knew this was true, because she had struggled mightily with Tyler's previous refusal to ask her out. The sole reason she had managed to wait was because Zach had insisted that it was only a matter of time, and that she just needed to be patient. Morgan had no such assurances about Bob.

"She has. Making posts that annoy Bob is just something to do when she's not at work."

"Interesting hobby," Tyler commented.

"Maybe, but I'm thinking about what Jeffrey said. If Morgan is in San Francisco to find someone else, having a bunch of social media posts about her fabulous single life there certainly won't hurt," Kelsey said.

"And she can irritate Bob in the process. That makes sense."

"I'm sure that she thinks he started it, with all the women on his yacht."

"Yeah, I guess he did. To be fair, that used to be his normal life."

"Used to be?" Kelsey asked curiously.

"Before he met Morgan Hill," Tyler clarified.

There was something amusing to Kelsey about the fact that it was three p.m. and they hadn't managed to eat lunch yet. But finally, they were sitting in a cafe two blocks from their hotel, looking at the menu.

"What are you having?" Tyler asked her.

"A panini, I think," Kelsey said.

"Hungry?"

"Starving."

"It's all that exercise," Tyler commented.

Kelsey smiled at him. "Beats running," she replied. "Although I should probably do that too."

"We can go to the gym tomorrow morning," Tyler said.

"You'll go with me?"

"Of course. I have to exercise in order to keep up with my bride."

"You're doing fine," Kelsey said, putting her menu aside. "But I'd love to work out with you."

Tyler looked thoughtful for a moment.

"I have an idea," he said brightly.

Kelsey's eyes sparkled with delight an hour later.

"We have time to play?" she asked excitedly.

"Sure," Tyler replied.

"Race you to the swings!" Kelsey said, and she dashed off. Tyler had brought her to Castel Sant Angelo, and after looking at the museum inside, they had walked to the park behind it.

Kelsey sat in one of the swings, and Tyler held onto it to push her. He gave her hair a kiss, pulled the swing back, and let go.

Hours later, after their trip to the Forum, and a late dinner at an excellent family-style pasta restaurant, Kelsey and Tyler walked into the hotel lobby.

"Buona sera, Signor Olsen," the concierge said as they neared his desk. "This arrived for you." He handed Tyler a small box.

Tyler glanced at the label and smiled.

"Grazie," he replied.

"Prego. Buona sera, Signora Olsen," the concierge replied. Kelsey gave him a smile as Tyler led her to the elevator.

"What did you get?" Kelsey said as they took the elevator up.

"It's for you," Tyler replied.

"For me? What is it?" Kelsey asked.

"You'll see inside," Tyler replied.

Once they were in their room, sitting down on the sofa, Tyler handed Kelsey the small box. It had been shipped next-day air from Seattle. Kelsey opened it carefully and removed the bubble wrap from one of the five objects inside. Her eyes widened as she saw what was inside.

"Nail polish?" she said, holding up a bottle.

"Non-toxic nail polish," Tyler corrected.

Kelsey looked at him in confusion.

"It comes off with water. It's safe enough to put on Allie."

"Really?" Kelsey said, looking at the bottle. It was a deep, beautiful red.

"I don't want you using anything toxic on your body," Tyler said, removing another one of the bottles and unwrapping it. It was a sparkling gold. He handed the bottle to Kelsey.

"Tyler, everyone uses nail polish," Kelsey protested.

"You don't. Not any more," Tyler said firmly. "Neither does Jess. Ryan replaced all of hers as well."

Kelsey looked at Tyler, and he kissed her on the lips.

"Camille said that this is the brand that Lisa uses, and every color they make will be waiting for you at home," Tyler continued. He brushed a strand of Kelsey's blonde hair with his hand. "I want you to be healthy."

"Thank you, Tyler," Kelsey said, beaming.

As Kelsey lay in Tyler's arms that night, she watched him as he slept and felt his gentle breathing. Kelsey had to admit that she was fascinated by him.

Kelsey knew that Tyler worried that somehow in the rush of life, he would forget that Kelsey was important to him. But as Kelsey looked at Tyler in the darkness, Kelsey knew deep in her heart that it wasn't true. Tomorrow they would visit Tactec Roma, and Tyler would once again need to be focused and working. He had so many things that he was responsible for, so many things to do — yet he had noticed something as small as his wife's nail polish.

Kelsey knew, as she lay in Tyler's arms, that she was loved.

The pretty receptionist with long brown hair and bright eyes behind fashionable glasses greeted Tyler immediately. It was clear that she had been waiting for them.

"Buon giorno, Signor Olsen," she said briskly.

Kelsey watched as Tyler responded in what seemed to her flawless Italian. As the receptionist called back to someone in the office on her phone, Kelsey wondered when Tyler had found the time to learn a fourth language.

"Welcome, welcome," said a voice a moment later. A fashionable man, who seemed in his mid-40s, came around the corner to greet them. "Tyler, it's good to see you again," he said.

"Hi, Lorenzo. This is my wife, Kelsey."

"Hi," Kelsey said, extending her hand.

Lorenzo shook it gently. "Come, I want to show you the office," he said, gesturing to them.

Kelsey looked around curiously as they followed Lorenzo into the main office. She hadn't spent a lot of time in Tactec offices, despite her long relationship with Tyler. She had been to the floor where Jeffrey and Jessica worked, but Kelsey knew that it wasn't designed like most of the offices at Tactec, and was mostly used for overflow staff, like interns and new employees who hadn't been assigned a desk yet. Kelsey had also seen Lisa Olsen's office, but of course, that wasn't standard Tactec design either. Kelsey hadn't seen Tyler's desk, because even though he had worked for Tactec since May, he still didn't have one. He was shuttling from department to department on an almost-daily basis.

The office was bright and comfortably designed. It felt something like a modern home, with comfy sofas, large worktables and lots of cozy touches. Because Kelsey had visited a few startups, she knew that this design style was quite common in the tech world. With long hours, most tech companies found that a little more money invested in a comfortable workspace led to more productive employees.

"We're a small office," Lorenzo said. "Only 50 people work here in Rome, and at least half of them are out on the road visiting clients today."

"Clients?" Kelsey asked.

"The staff here are mostly marketing and sales," Tyler commented. "Additionally, we've bought two startups which are run out of this office."

"Oh," Kelsey said. When she thought of Tactec she usually thought of the engineers. But of course, they needed to sell their products as well.

"How is your mother? We haven't seen her for quite a while," Lorenzo continued.

"She's fine. She's only left the country three times this year," Tyler said diplomatically.

"Yes, she's very busy," Lorenzo agreed. "We know she's thinking of us, because Mr. Perkins visits us quite regularly."

"Bob tries to come to Europe at least twice a year, but it's getting a bit more difficult as we grow," Tyler said.

"I will be going to Seattle next month, along with Alessia," Lorenzo said.

"Lisa is having a 'Head of Country' conference for the managing directors of all the offices outside the US," Tyler explained to Kelsey. "It's the only way she can keep track of what's going on."

"How many countries does Tactec have offices in?" Kelsey asked.

"One hundred and thirty-seven," Lorenzo said promptly.

Kelsey looked at Tyler in disbelief.

"It's a big company," he shrugged.

As Lorenzo led them around the office, Kelsey was fascinated by some of the things that he pointed out. In the kitchen, there was a pull-out wine cooler. Like many startups she had seen, the office had an open-plan layout, but what was interesting to her was that there were several large tables in the middle of the space, along with a row of small desks facing the windows. All but one of the desks was empty.

"These are our hot desks," Lorenzo said, gesturing to them. "When our sales team members need a place to work, they just take one. They're unassigned."

"That's what I use too," Tyler commented to Kelsey.

"The large tables are used by all the teams for meetings," Lorenzo continued.

"Doesn't it get noisy?" Tyler asked.

"Of course. But it's good because there are very few secrets," Lorenzo replied. "We do also have two conference rooms when privacy is preferred. We'll use one of them for this afternoon's user test. Will you be able to join us?" Lorenzo said hopefully.

Tyler glanced at Kelsey, and she read the look in his eyes. Although Tyler had agreed to spend 90 minutes at Tactec Roma with Lisa, it was clear that Lorenzo had something else in mind.

"It's fine," she answered. Kelsey knew that Tyler was in a tough spot, so she didn't mind if he needed to work today.

"Wonderful. We're on our eighth iteration for our newest app, and the design team is really hoping for some good feedback this time so they can release a beta version," Lorenzo said.

"What's the app?" Tyler asked.

"This one is for the car-sharing team," Lorenzo replied. Kelsey knew from talking to Tyler that of the two startups based in the Rome office, one was a car-sharing company, and the other was a shopping app, both focused on the Italian market. The shopping app had a sister office in Milan, Italy's fashion capital, which was also considered part of Tactec Roma.

Kelsey wondered what an 'iteration' was as she held Tyler's hand and they walked around the large office. She didn't want to ask, as Lorenzo excitedly talked about the office and the plans for the business with Tyler, and she also couldn't help but wonder if she should know as an attorney focusing on intellectual property. She wouldn't be embarrassed to ask Tyler, but she hoped that it would be explained during the day.

At eleven, Kelsey and Tyler joined the team members who were in the office for a meeting at one of the large tables. Kelsey and Tyler sat in seats, as did some of the staff, while others stood around the table. It felt very casual to Kelsey, so she assumed that they had this type of check-in meeting every day.

"In honor of our guests, we'll practice our English today," Lorenzo said. Looking around, Kelsey could tell that the staff was completely unconcerned about this request. However, one person said something in Italian, and Lorenzo looked at Tyler, who answered.

"Kelsey doesn't work for Tactec, however she is bound by the Tactec confidentiality agreement, and won't disclose anything outside of the company. You can say anything in front of her," Tyler said. Kelsey glanced at him, and he smiled. In fact, Kelsey knew that she hadn't signed anything that required her to be silent about Tactec information, but of course, she wouldn't say anything about what she had heard. She appreciated Tyler's trust in her.

"Excellent," Lorenzo said. "Let's continue."

Kelsey and Tyler sat quietly as various announcements were made. People reported on upcoming customer visits, and on new business deals. Tyler stroked Kelsey's hand with his thumb as they sat.

"Thank you," Lorenzo said once the final speaker was finished. "Before we get back to work, are there any questions for Tyler? It's not every day that we have a visitor from the home office."

"Has the company decided where the new European head office is going to be?" a man with dark hair and a neatly-cut suit asked. "Ever since Brexit, it's been clear that we need to move our headquarters out of London and into the EU, but nothing has happened yet," he added.

The expression on Tyler's face didn't change, but Kelsey guessed that he was unhappy about the question. When the United Kingdom had voted to leave the European Union, a lot of businesses had rethought their European strategies, and decided to move their European headquarters out of the UK, to maintain their relationships with EU countries. Tactec, however, had been dragging its heels. Kelsey was sure that Tyler had an opinion about where the next headquarters should be, but as in all things dealing with Tactec, all Tyler could do was make suggestions and hope that they would be implemented. At least until Tyler became CEO.

"I believe that there is still some internal debate about the question," Tyler said. "I don't have an update."

"Rome is perfect for the new EU headquarters," Lorenzo said boldly. "Please go back to Seattle and tell the CEO that."

"She'll want to know why," Tyler replied simply. Kelsey knew by Tyler's tone that he was giving Lorenzo a chance to make the best case possible at this moment. Lorenzo took the bait.

"Rome is an incredible startup hub," he said. "If we want to grow as a company, we need to focus on building connections with some of the bright young people who are going to shape the digital future. Rome is the place to make that happen."

"Good," Tyler said non-commitally. "When I get back to Seattle, I'll find out more about what the company's considering."

Kelsey didn't have to be married to Tyler to know that Lorenzo's best argument had clearly failed to influence Tyler. She could tell that Lorenzo knew it too.

"Are there any other questions?" Lorenzo asked the team.

Once the meeting was over at noon, Kelsey and Tyler were escorted to one of the two conference rooms.

"Wait here. We'll get started in a few minutes. Can I get you something to drink? Water? Hot chocolate?" Kelsey's ears perked up.

"Hot chocolate would be great," Tyler said. "You too, Kels?"

Kelsey nodded happily, and Lorenzo left the room.

"Thank you for your patience," Tyler said, giving her a kiss.

"It's fine. It's only one day," Kelsey replied.

"I'd like us to leave after the user test, but I think we're going to be invited to lunch."

"Tyler, it's fine," Kelsey said.

"Thank you," Tyler repeated.

"So what are we about to do?" Kelsey asked curiously. She wasn't sure what happened in a user test."

"Of course, maybe this is new to you," Tyler said. "In a software company like Tactec, there are several different things that have to happen before a product is released to the public. We start with an idea, for example, we decide to build a car-sharing app. A lot of people would assume that the important part of that is the job of the engineers, because they are the ones who write the code to allow the app to function. But a really important part of the work is done by the User Experience team, who talk to customers, and who design what you see and read on the screen. The best-coded app is meaningless if people can't use it, and that's what we'll be working on today. Our job is to sit and listen to the customer and hear what they think about our product."

"So what's an iteration?" Kelsey asked. The term hadn't come up again, and she was still curious.

"In Tactec, someone has an idea. We make something. Usually, we don't make the entire app, but we might make something that has the basic design, some of the features, without actually doing the coding necessary to make it work."

"A prototype," Kelsey said, summing up Tyler's words in her mind.

"Right. We take that prototype to some testers. Sometimes we test internally, among the staff, other times we get actual Tactec customers or potential customers. We give them the prototype and ask them, what do you like about this? What don't you like? Does this satisfy your needs? And they tell us. We take their feedback, and put it into another prototype. And test it again. Each time we run through that cycle we call it an iteration."

"Oh," Kelsey said, understanding. "So this has happened eight times? Is that a lot?"

Tyler shook his head. "Not really."

"What would be?"

"Fifty iterations?"

"Isn't that expensive?" Kelsey asked.

"We try to keep the costs down," Tyler replied. "That's why we try to work out as many problems as we can before someone starts working on coding."

"But you have to create these prototypes and do interviews."

"True. But UX designers have tools that help them make prototypes quickly, and our user researchers have a lot of experience in guiding users to give us the information that we need. That's why it's rare to have fifty iterations of a product. In that case, it probably means that either the staff isn't listening to customer feedback, or the market for the product isn't really there."

"UX designers?"

"UX means user experience. Their job is to think about how a customer will use the screens and to design them."

"Why haven't I met any of these people?" Kelsey asked. She had visited several startups, but invariably met with the founders or occasionally engineers.

Tyler laughed. "The last person they want to meet is a lawyer," he said. "Legal is always telling them that they have to add disclaimers or change words in the product. A UX designer wants to create the simplest flow possible. Lawyers can get in the way of that. Also," Tyler mused, "lawyers often slow up the process. We can go from prototype to sellable product in weeks. You and I both know that a two-page contract can sit on a lawyer's desk for that long."

"That's because we do a thorough job," Kelsey said. She bristled at the implication that lawyers slowed down business.

"Obviously, I'm not judging lawyers, Kels. I'm just telling you how we're perceived in the process."

"So legal isn't usually involved in the UX process?"

"Not if they can help it."

"But Lisa's a lawyer. So is Bob."

"Both of them close their eyes when it comes to what's being created in their names. Their motto is, 'Legal will get involved when we get sued.'"

"Really?"

"I've sat in on some of the design meetings. They are legal minefields," Tyler said simply. Kelsey lifted an eyebrow, but Tyler shook his head. "You don't want to know," he said.

Lorenzo walked back in, accompanied by a young woman with a bright-blonde ponytail, who was carrying a sleek Tactec laptop. Lorenzo placed cups of steaming hot chocolate in front of both Tyler and Kelsey.

"The tester is here. Let's begin," he said, as the woman plugged her laptop into the large screen monitor hanging on the wall.

As Kelsey and Tyler sipped their cocoa, they watched on the big screen as the tester walked into what seemed to be a small office with a cozy sofa, and was greeted by someone that Kelsey assumed was the user researcher whom Tyler had described. They both sat on the sofa. The researcher picked up a Tactec phone that was sitting on the coffee table in front of the sofa, and began chatting in Italian. Thanks to the camera that was in the room where the test was happening, they could see everything that was happening on the phone in the testing room, and the tester's hands as he interacted with the prototype.

Kelsey watched in fascination as the tester pressed buttons and scrolled through the app. It was interesting to see how the app worked, even though she couldn't understand the conversation between the tester and the researcher.

"We've asked them to try to arrange a booking here in Rome," Lorenzo commented as the tester continued to scroll through the app on screen.

"He seems to be stuck," the woman in the ponytail commented. "Wait, he's figured it out," she said. She made a note in her computer.

Lorenzo frowned. "I'm not sure that we've designed the best first-time experience."

The woman glanced at him. "Now you say something," she commented.

Lorenzo laughed. "I say something all the time, but you designers never listen."

"You aren't a Tactec customer," the woman replied, which seemed to finish the argument. Lorenzo turned his attention back to the screen.

"Why do they have to put their phone number in at this point?" Tyler asked. "Why isn't it reading it off the phone?"

"In this version, we ask for an additional phone number where the customer can be contacted. It's under discussion, because a lot of us think it's an unnecessary step."

"I agree," Tyler said, looking back at the screen. The woman made another note in her computer. Kelsey suspected that any comments from the CEO's son would be taken seriously. Obviously, it was being taken more seriously than the input from the head of the office.

The tester continued to work through the app, stopping every so often to ask questions or point to the app and make a comment.

"What is he concerned about?" Tyler asked during a particularly long interlude.

"He thinks that we should have luxury cars as one of our vehicle types," Lorenzo said. "We've actually gotten this feedback before, but the problem is that we don't have a lot of clarity about how to define a 'luxury car' within our data set. If you drive a Fiat, you think that a

149

BMW is a luxury car, but if you drive a BMW, only a Maserati will do. And we get complaints whether we narrow the field too much, or expand it too much. So we decided to eliminate it."

"I see," Tyler said, turning back to the screen. Lorenzo and the woman looked at each other, but were silent. Kelsey found the interactions between them and Tyler interesting, in fact almost more interesting than what was on screen. In Seattle, senior-level Tactec employees weren't deferential to Tyler, not by a long shot. They were unafraid to express their views, as had been demonstrated by the events at the Tactec picnic. Here, there seemed to be a little confusion about how to respond to Tyler's presence. He was the representative of the CEO, but he was also clearly junior to the head of the Italian office. Or was he? Although they seemed to be having trouble figuring it out, Kelsey had no doubt who was actually more important to the future of the Italian office. It was the man with Lisa Olsen's number on his phone under the contact name 'Mom'.

Kelsey thought about this as the tester selected his car on the screen. From the outside, Tactec looked like a lot of companies. A money-generating enterprise focused on its shareholders. But Kelsey knew that although it might seem that business decisions were made in a cold, calculating manner, the reality of Tactec was that only one person's voice really mattered.

Lisa Olsen's.

But Kelsey, Lisa, and probably only a handful of people knew that there was another person who had the power to change Lisa's mind. And that was Tyler.

When it came to Tactec, Tyler was clearly the power behind the throne. Kelsey knew that Tyler didn't think so, because he was impatient to see change happen. However, over time, Kelsey had realized that slowly, everything that Tyler wanted, Tyler got.

From Lisa Olsen's perspective, it probably made perfect sense. Tyler was going to be CEO soon, sooner perhaps than he thought. Giving into his vision of the company now would help lay the groundwork for him in the future.

And as Kelsey looked at her husband as he drank his hot chocolate and watched the screen, she knew that without a doubt that he had a vision for Tactec. The only question was, how would he be able to convince Tactec's employees that his vision was the right one for the company? Now, everyone looked up to Lisa Olsen. But her son? Kelsey knew that there was work to do. It was why she was spending a day of her honeymoon in a Tactec office in the middle of Rome.

There was a little commotion on screen as the researcher stood up. They watched as she walked across the screen.

"Not bad," Lorenzo commented.

"It could be better," the woman said.

Suddenly, the researcher opened the door to the room and stuck her head in.

"Did any of you have questions for the tester?" she asked.

"Can you ask him how he would define a luxury car?" Tyler asked.

"Of course," she said. "Anything else?" Everyone else in the room shook their heads, and she stepped back out. A moment later she was back on screen, chatting with the tester. After an another couple of minutes, the tester waved at the camera, then he stood up and left.

"He knew we were watching?" Kelsey asked.

"Yes," Tyler said as the researcher walked back into the room and sat in one of the chairs.

"So the tester said we should use the same categories as car rental places do," she said.

"What are those?" Lorenzo asked the woman with the ponytail.

"Non lo so, Googl'are," she said, and despite the language barrier, Kelsey could hear her testiness. Tyler and the researcher laughed.

"She told him to Google it." Tyler whispered to Kelsey. Kelsey suppressed her own giggle.

Lorenzo leaned back in his chair. "So we got better feedback this time."

"Much better," the researcher agreed.

The woman, who Kelsey had figured out was the UX designer, frowned. "I think we need another round."

"No, we need to release this. No amount of further user testing is going to make a difference. We need the public to comment," Lorenzo said. "It's time to beta."

The UX designer looked at Tyler. "What do you think, Tyler?" she asked, clearly hoping for another vote on her side. "The beta will have the Tactec name."

"Ms. Olsen always says to get it done and move on to the next thing," Tyler replied. "Once it's in beta, our customers will let us know what we've done wrong."

"Exactly," Lorenzo said firmly."We'll make the few changes he suggested, and put it out there." The designer sighed unhappily.

"It's time to let the baby graduate," the researcher teased.

"It's not your baby," the designer said, and Kelsey realized why she was so disappointed. She was probably not only the UX designer, but also the founder of the startup that was now based in this office. Once their meeting was over, and they had finished discussing what they had heard and seen, Kelsey included, she decided to ask Tyler.

"Yes, Martina sold the company to Tactec," he confirmed. "She and her co-founder felt that they were in over their head because of the potential liabilities involved in car sharing, so they sold themselves to Tactec. We've partnered with an Italian insurance company, and now it's just a matter of finishing the app."

"I'm surprised she doesn't want to release the app yet. It seems OK."

"I guess she's a perfectionist," Tyler shrugged.

Lorenzo re-entered the room. He had left with the other staff members after the meeting. "Will you be able to join us for lunch?" he asked brightly.

"Of course," Tyler said, and Kelsey gave him a smile.

Tyler, Kelsey, and ten other Tactec employees headed over to a small trattoria near the office. They were seated quickly, and it was clear to Kelsey that this was a routine.

"We called ahead," Lorenzo said to Tyler, as glasses of wine were poured. Kelsey and Tyler declined theirs.

"Poor Martina," someone cooed.

"Pasta will make you feel better," the user researcher said. Martina continued to frown.

"What do you think we should do?" Tyler asked Kelsey, who turned her attention back to him. "Release it in beta or not?"

Kelsey thought for a moment. "Well, as your lawyer, I would say that you should make sure that everything is perfect before you do, but I'm getting the sense that the tech industry isn't run the same way a law firm is," she replied. "This explains a lot of my clients," she mused.

Tyler laughed. "Your job is to rein them in," he said.

"But at Tactec, there doesn't seem to be anyone around to do that," Kelsey noted.

"We like it like that," Tyler replied.

"I thought you went to law school," Kelsey teased. "You're supposed to be on my side."

"My idealism was beaten out of me during my first month at Tactec. Now I'm just grateful when an engineer isn't taking other people's code and putting it into his own."

"Do people do that?" Kelsey asked. Tyler looked at her innocently.

"Never mind. I don't want to know." Kelsey said.

"Good artists copy. Great artists steal," Tyler said. "A quote from Picasso."

"I'm not listening to you," Kelsey replied.

"We're married now. You can't testify against me," Tyler said, stroking her shoulders.

Kelsey laughed. "The real reason you married me," she teased.

To her surprise, Tyler bit his lip. "Not even close, Princess," he replied, surveying her.

"Lunch was nice," Kelsey said two hours later as they walked in the Italian sunshine. They had eaten Kelsey's favorite spaghetti carbonara — although this version was made with fresh tuna and eggplant — and they had had a spirited discussion with the staff. Every employee felt that the logical place to put Tactec's new European headquarters was in Rome, and like the Tactec staff in Seattle, they hadn't been hesitant to tell Tyler their thoughts. In fact, Kelsey thought that Lorenzo wanted a further chance to try to convince Tyler, but Tyler had reminded him that they would leave Rome the next day. Tyler had refrained from telling Lorenzo that the couple would be back in Rome before they returned to Seattle.

"I was looking forward to going to the Vatican," Tyler groused.

"We can go tomorrow, before our train," Kelsey said.

Tyler kissed her hair. "Always an optimist," Tyler replied.

"Worst case, we can go when we come back," Kelsey said.

"True," Tyler said.

"It's fine. Think of it this way — the money that Tactec has made is the reason we're here in the first place."

"As lawyers we could have afforded to honeymoon in Rome," Tyler said.

"Not in our current hotel room," Kelsey pointed out.

"All we need is a bed, Princess," Tyler replied. "Speaking of," he said, letting the words linger.

Kelsey looked up at his sexy eyes.

"I could use some exercise," she replied breathlessly.

An hour later, Kelsey was lying on her back, boiling hot and attempting to catch her breath. Tyler leaned over and kissed her lips. Kelsey looked up at him, her breath coming back in deep gasps. Suddenly Tyler's phone rang.

"Don't answer it," Kelsey commanded.

"OK," Tyler said, kissing her again.

Kelsey lay in the soft sheets, as she basked in the glow of Tyler's magic. Tyler ran his fingers along her collarbone and kissed her shoulder. Kelsey smiled.

The phone rang again.

"Who is it?" Kelsey demanded. She knew that the phone that Tyler had brought to Italy had separate ringtones for all of the approved callers. And it had nothing else. No apps, no camera. The only thing that Tyler's top-end Tactec smartphone could do was make calls and receive text messages. Everything else had been wiped from the phone by Sergei, to comply with Tactec's rule that company information could not be taken across the US border on electronic devices.

"It's Lorenzo. He's going to keep ringing until I answer, I think." Tyler said.

Kelsey sighed in irritation. "Fine, but tell him to hurry up. You're mine now."

Tyler laughed as he picked up the phone. "I'll let him know," he said. *"Ciao Lorenzo,"* he continued, taking the call. Kelsey shifted on the pillow as she waited for Tyler to return.

"What?" Tyler said, sitting up in bed.

Kelsey looked at him questioningly, but Tyler had turned away from her.

"But…" Tyler began, then he stopped."Fine, OK. It's fine," he said. "Of course, I understand. 11 a.m. OK. *Ciao,*" And with that Tyler hung up the phone. It took him a moment to set the phone on the nightstand and return to Kelsey. He slid his arm under her warm back as he lay next to her.

"What's going on?" Kelsey asked in concern.

"I've been set up," Tyler said.

"What are you talking about?"

"Somehow the mayor of Rome has found out that I'm in town, and he's invited me and Lorenzo to come to city hall tomorrow so he can tell me how great Rome would be as the next European home of Tactec."

Kelsey's mouth dropped open in shock.

Tyler lifted an eyebrow. "Interesting coincidence, isn't it?"

"Oh, Tyler," Kelsey said in sympathy.

"You're invited too. The mayor knows I'm on my honeymoon," Tyler said. "Honestly, if they would just let me enjoy my vacation, I'd have plenty of nice things to say to Lisa about Rome."

Kelsey smiled and stroked Tyler's chest.

"It's hard being Tyler Olsen," she teased.

"Are you being sarcastic?" Tyler challenged her.

Kelsey nodded. "I am. What are you going to do about it?"

Tyler grinned. "I'm going to show you how hard it can be," he replied.

Hours later, Kelsey and Tyler were cuddled together on the sofa. Kelsey wore her black silk robe. and her feet were intertwined with Tyler's as they ate pizza which had been delivered from one of Rome's corner pizzerias. It was delicious, and Kelsey was trying to be careful to make sure she didn't get any on her robe.

"I can't believe that I'm eating an anchovy," Tyler said, right before Kelsey put another into his mouth.

"They're fried," she said, taking another bite of pizza. "Almost everything is better fried."

"This is the same woman who woke me up to go to the gym this morning."

"I'm looking for balance in my life, Tyler. Moderation."

"I see," Tyler said. He leaned his head onto Kelsey's shoulder and sighed happily. "Thanks for coming with me tomorrow."

"I don't mind. It might be interesting. It was today."

"No, it wasn't."

"It was for me. Anyway, I just like being with you. I don't care what we do," Kelsey replied.

"That's good," Tyler commented. "Because I'm confident more of my days will look like this in the future."

"Probably," Kelsey agreed.

"Maybe I should get rid of my phone for the rest of the trip," Tyler mused.

"You can't. Suppose someone needs you?"

"Who? Ryan?"

"We leave Rome tomorrow," Kelsey said, and there was a little excitement in her voice, because they were going to take the train to Florence. "So at least you won't get any more work calls."

"I guess you have a point," Tyler said. "This just isn't turning out to be as relaxing as I expected."

"It's fine," Kelsey said. She rubbed his ankle with her foot. "At least we've had plenty of time together."

"That's true. There are places I wanted to take you, though," Tyler said.

"Are you disappointed that we can't go to the Vatican tomorrow?" Kelsey asked curiously. Thanks to the Mayor's invitation in the morning, their trip would have to wait. Their train to Florence was scheduled for 3 p.m.

"We can go when we come back. We have time," Tyler replied. He opened his mouth, and Kelsey placed another fried anchovy into it. Tyler's phone rang again, this time from the bedroom where he had left it. But it was a different ring than before. At this point, Kelsey knew the ringtone of Lorenzo's calls.

Tyler stood up quickly.

"It's Conor," he said, and he dashed into the other room. Kelsey ate pizza as she waited for Tyler to return. She wondered how many ringtones Tyler had memorized. She also wondered what was going on, but Tyler wasn't talking, he was listening. She finished her slice and had moved on to another one, before Tyler came back into the room. He looked unhappy.

"Security is coming up," he said quietly. "The paparazzi is outside."

Kelsey waited in the bedroom as Tyler spoke Italian to the head of hotel security in their suite's living room a few minutes later. She felt terrible, because although she wasn't particularly upset, she was sure that Tyler was. She heard the front door shut, then Tyler said,

"You can come out now."

Kelsey walked back out into the living room. She was still wearing her silk robe, but Tyler had got dressed to greet security. Kelsey stood on her toes and kissed Tyler's lips.

"I'm so sorry, Kelsey," he said in frustration.

"What's going on?"

"Someone in the mayor's office sent out a press release that he would be meeting with me tomorrow to discuss the possibility of Tactec's relocation. That seems to have set off a search to figure out where we were staying, and it didn't take too long to find us."

"Oh, boy," Kelsey said. She wasn't a fan of the paparazzi, having been their target a couple of times.

"So they're camped out on the Spanish Steps," Tyler continued. "Conor called to inform me that you and I aren't allowed to take the train to Florence tomorrow, we'll have to be driven."

"Really?" Kelsey said in disappointment.

"It's going to add an hour to the trip. I'm sorry, Kelsey."

"It's not your fault, Tyler," Kelsey said.

"Conor said if things calm down, we can take the other two trains," Kelsey nodded. They had planned to take trains each time they changed cities, but she knew that there was nothing that they could do. Their safety was important, and it would be terrible if they were followed to Florence by the paparazzi. Their honeymoon, which had already been disrupted, might be cancelled altogether if there were more issues. Kelsey didn't want to have to return home early.

"It's fine. We'll snuggle in the back seat of the car," Kelsey said positively. Tyler gave her a hug. She felt happy in his strong arms.

"Thank you for being so understanding," Tyler said. "On the plus side, security brought up our clothes for tomorrow."

"We have to have special clothes? I guess we do," Kelsey said, answering her own question. For the trip she had packed casual clothes so they could blend in with the backpacker crowd as they traveled from place to place. She also had three elegant dresses for the dinners that Tyler had arranged for them, and of course, she had the chic travel outfits she wore and would wear while traveling through the airports. But there was nothing in her luggage that was suitable for meeting the mayor of Rome. "Did Jeffrey arrange for them? Is he in Rome?"

"Yes and no. He arranged the clothes for us, but he's not leaving Punta Ala without a reason."

"Where is Punta Ala?" Kelsey asked.

"It's a seaside resort a couple of hours from Florence," Tyler said. He released Kelsey from his arms and led her back to the sofa. They resumed their positions there, Kelsey's feet balanced on top of Tyler's.

"Want a cold fried anchovy?" she asked.

"Yes," Tyler said opening his mouth. He chewed thoughtfully. "Tastes the same," he commented.

"Good. The paparazzi can't ruin our day," she said.

"You have a point," Tyler said thoughtfully. "I think we should go to the Vatican tomorrow, after we go to city hall. If we aren't taking the train, we don't have to leave Rome early."

"That would be great," Kelsey said happily. She knew how much Tyler wanted to see the Vatican Museum, and she didn't want him to have to wait for almost two weeks to do that.

"You have such a good attitude about life," Tyler said. "I should learn from you."

"I'm married to the most wonderful person in the world. Why wouldn't I have a good attitude?" Kelsey asked, taking a bite of her pizza and looking at him. Tyler's eyes sparkled in the light, and he smiled at her.

"There is no one in the world I would rather go through things like this with," Tyler said. "But I want you to have fun too."

"I am having fun, Tyler. Life is an adventure, and I get to share that adventure with you," Tyler wrapped his arms around Kelsey's waist and hugged her gently. She replied with a kiss.

Kelsey wanted to return to the hotel gym the next morning, and once again, Tyler joined her. After a long run on the treadmill, she wiped the sweat off her face with one of the hotel's soft towels and walked over to where Tyler was lifting weights. His muscular arms glistened as he sat on the bench.

"Are you done?" Tyler asked as she leaned down to give him a kiss.

"We should do sit-ups," Kelsey said. "There are a set of kettlebells over there."

Tyler gave her a look.

"Doing sit-ups with kettlebells wasn't in my wedding vows," he said.

"Oh, come on. It's your favorite exercise," Kelsey teased. In fact, she knew that Tyler hated it.

"I think you know what my favorite exercise is, Mrs. Olsen," Tyler replied, as he scanned Kelsey's body.

"Second favorite, then," Kelsey cooed. She held out her hand and pulled Tyler up from the bench. She waited for him as he returned his weights to the rack, then they walked over to the rack of kettlebells together.

"Twenty pounds?" Kelsey asked.

"Are you sure you can handle twenty?"

"Is that a dare?" Kelsey said.

"No, I'm serious. I don't want you to get injured."

Kelsey nodded. "We'll do eighteen," she said.

Tyler took an eighteen-pound kettlebell off the rack as Kelsey lay down on her towel, which cushioned her from the hard gym floor. She looked up at Tyler.

"We could do something else together with you in that position," Tyler commented.

"Not here we can't," Kelsey replied. "Stop stalling."

Tyler sat on his towel, his ankles touching Kelsey's.

"How many of these are we going to do?" he asked.

"One hundred," Kelsey replied.

"Seriously, Kels."

"Two hundred, then," Kelsey said.

"I'll do ten."

"It's not worth doing if we only do ten," Kelsey replied.

"Then I can put this away," Tyler said, motioning to stand.

"Fifty. And get back here."

"You're so bossy," Tyler commented.

"Only in the gym," Kelsey replied. "And in bed."

"You aren't bossy in bed," Tyler said.

"You don't think so?"

"No. You're demanding. There's a difference."

"Hardly. You're stalling again. Let's do this," Kelsey said.

Tyler leaned back on his towel, and holding the kettlebell in his hands, did a sit-up.

"One," Kelsey said, taking the kettlebell from him. She lay back down and did a sit-up of her own, the kettlebell now in her own hands.

"What's the difference between demanding and bossy?" Kelsey asked as Tyler took the kettlebell from her.

"Weren't you supposed to say two?" Tyler said, as he did his sit-up.

"I'll say two when it's my turn again," Kelsey replied. "What's the difference?"

"Here," Tyler said, handing her the kettlebell. "Demanding is having high standards. Bossy is ordering others to live up to those standards."

Kelsey did her sit-up, and handed the kettlebell to Tyler.

"Two," she said. "I see. So you don't mind when I'm demanding in bed?" she asked.

Tyler did his sit-up, and handed the kettlebell to Kelsey.

"Do we really need to have this conversation now?" he asked.

"Yes," Kelsey said as she lay back. "Answer the question, counsel."

"No, I like knowing what you like when we're in bed together. I want to please you," Tyler replied.

Kelsey felt herself blush as she sat back up.

"You always do," she admitted as she handed Tyler the kettlebell.

"Three," Tyler said.

"Three," Kelsey said, and Tyler lay back, kettlebell in hand.

"Do I please you?" she asked. Tyler sighed from the floor.

"Yes. This is ten times worse when we're talking."

"I'm trying to distract you."

"It's not working."

Tyler sat up and handed her the kettlebell.

"Can I be doing anything else for you?" Kelsey asked as she lay back.

"I could use some quiet for the next few minutes," Tyler teased.

"Something else," Kelsey said, sitting up again.

"No. You're perfect," Tyler said as he took the kettlebell. "Even now."

Kelsey declined Tyler's offer to shower together when they returned to their room. As she took her turn in the bathroom, she thought she heard the front door open, then close. Once she was dried and wrapped in her own silk robe, she peeked her head out of the bedroom.

"Can I come out?" she asked.

"Yes. It was room service," Tyler said. Kelsey walked out of the bedroom. "We aren't allowed out of our hotel room any more," he added.

"It's fine. I like having breakfast on the terrace," Kelsey said.

"You might want to put something else on when you go out there today," Tyler commented.

"You don't think they can see us up here, do you?" Kelsey said.

"All it takes is a drone with a camera," Tyler replied.

Kelsey sighed. "I'll be back," she said, returning to the bedroom.

They had a leisurely breakfast on the terrace, with nothing bare but their feet. They fed each other omelets and granola parfaits and talked about all of the things that they had seen in Rome. Kelsey knew that Tyler was disappointed that work had followed him across the globe, but she knew that it was a preview of their lives together. Kelsey felt that if she could accept the small interruptions now, she would be able to accept the much bigger distractions later, when Tyler was CEO. And in her mind, it was fine.

Kelsey understood, perhaps in a way that Tyler didn't, that there were always trade-offs in life. A price had to be paid for every decision. Tyler was still having trouble accepting that his two-billion-dollar inheritance came with strings. As a member of the working class, Kelsey was surprised at how few strings the inheritance came with. But of course, Tyler was comparing himself to Ryan, whose inheritance seemingly came with no strings at all.

From Kelsey's point of view, a few hours of work carved out of their vacation was a small price to pay for three weeks in Italy. So as she put on the cashmere sweater that Jeffrey had sent over from the Prada boutique for her to wear, Kelsey reminded herself, that at least for her, there was only one thing for her to do over the next couple of hours. And that was to play the role of Mrs. Tyler Olsen.

Kelsey smiled but didn't look at the cameras as Tyler helped her into the hotel's town car a half-hour later. She settled herself into her seat, and put her safety belt on, her new camel-colored Prada bag nestled into the space next to the door. Tyler joined her in the back seat, and their bodyguard Marco — the latest addition to Tyler and Kelsey's vacation — sat in the front, next to the hotel's driver.

Tyler took Kelsey's hand and kissed it. Then he turned and looked glumly out of the window. Kelsey stroked his hand in sympathy. Thanks to Kelsey's newsfeed, which featured news about Tactec, they had found out that Tactec had put out a press release stating that Tyler was in Italy on Tactec business, but that no decisions had been made about where Tactec would move their European headquarters.

Instead of tamping down expectations, the vague press release had seemingly thrown gasoline on the fire of speculation. Kelsey's newsfeed was updating every few minutes with articles about why Tyler Olsen was meeting with the mayor of Rome, what Tactec would be doing in Europe, and where he would be traveling on behalf of Tactec next. The mayors of Paris, Brussels, and Berlin had all put out press releases of their own, inviting Tyler to come visit their beautiful, technology-focused, corporate-friendly cities, and Kelsey expected there would be many more. For now, however, they only had one mayor to meet.

The sleek town car drove them quickly through the Roman streets. Kelsey looked out the window at the many boutiques and cafes, more than a few of which they had managed to visit during their three free days in Rome. Kelsey felt that for Tyler, today felt like his second day of work, and in fact, she knew that he intended to bill his hours back to Tactec for the time they had spent. Kelsey suspected that Lisa Olsen wouldn't mind.

The meeting with the mayor was uneventful, although it was quite a bit longer than Kelsey expected. It began with a small surprise, as it turned out that Mrs. 'Rome's mayor' had been called into service to entertain Kelsey while the mayor and Tyler spoke privately at city hall. Silvia Rossi turned out to be delightful, complementing Kelsey's Prada outfit, while scolding her own husband for disrupting the Olsen couple's honeymoon.

Next there was a short press conference, where Tyler brilliantly outmaneuvered every attempt to pin him down on Tactec's next moves. As she watched, Kelsey thought that Becks would be very proud.

Finally, there were photos. Thousands of photos. The mayor and Tyler together. The mayor, Tyler, and their wives together. Tyler and the staff of city hall together. Lorenzo, who had come to city hall separately, managed to get into a few photographs, but it was clear that this time, it was Tyler's show. Lorenzo didn't seem to mind though. If the mayor managed to convince Tactec to move its European headquarters to Italy,

Lorenzo would be the first in line for a large promotion.

Tyler managed to escape an invitation to tea, insisting that he had promised his bride that they would visit the Vatican. With a gentle push from Silvia, the mayor said goodbye.

Freed from Tactec responsibilities, and with a new town car and driver, Kelsey and Tyler made their way to Vatican City. Jeffrey had arranged another tour guide for them, so they skipped the incredibly long line for the Vatican Museum and went inside.

"You didn't come here before?" Kelsey asked Tyler.

He shook his head. "We didn't have time. Lisa and I were only here for two days."

Kelsey didn't ask for details. Knowing her mother-in-law, Kelsey was confident that at least one of those days had been spent at the office in Rome. Lisa might have framed it as a trip so the teenaged Tyler could see Europe, but Kelsey had no doubt that it was really a trip to visit Tactec's European offices.

After what had just happened to Tyler, Kelsey supposed that it was inevitable. Any visit by the Tactec CEO would be noteworthy, since she had to spread her attention across 137 countries. Kelsey realized that the moment Tyler became CEO, he would be unlikely to be able to visit any country with a Tactec office without needing to work. It was something else Kelsey would need to prepare for.

The couple was stunned by the beautiful art in the museum. They kept pausing to look more closely at various works. Tyler knew many of the artists, and their tour guide gave them the details about the paintings and sculptures that they saw.

Once they walked out into the sunny courtyard, they discussed some of the things that they had seen.

"Did you notice the feet of the statues?" Kelsey asked Tyler.

"How worn they were? I noticed."

"I couldn't believe that so many people were touching the art. I saw at least three," Kelsey said.

"I guess for a lot of people it's more than art. There's the religious meaning as well," Tyler said.

Kelsey thought that he had a point. Jess had made a point of requesting to see the couple's photos from their visit to the Vatican. Jess had been as a child on a family visit to Italy, and she had commented on how beautiful the experience had been for her.

The couple and their guide went into the crowded Sistine Chapel and looked at the ceiling for a long time.

Kelsey was surprised that their next stop was an ATM, but she was shocked when Tyler chose Latin as the language. He took a picture of the screen before they left. Next, the guide led them to St. Peter's, which was ten times bigger than Kelsey could have imagined. Then he led them up to the top of the building. Once they arrived, Kelsey and Tyler stood there, holding hands and looking out at St. Peter's Square.

On their way out, as they were crossing St. Peter's Square, they got a surprise.

"Kelsey, look," Tyler said. The crowd around them was pointing.

It was the Pope.

"That was amazing!" Kelsey said, as they headed out of Rome. They were in the back of a large town car, their bodyguard Marco in the front, with a driver beside him.

"You liked Rome?"

"I loved Rome," Kelsey said.

"I'm sorry that you didn't get to see more of it."

"We'll see more on the trip back. Anyway, it was fun," Kelsey said, nuzzling against Tyler in the back seat. Tyler was quiet, then he said,

"I don't know how to apologize for letting work get in the way."

"You don't need to apologize," Kelsey said firmly. "Tyler, I love being with you. No matter what we're doing." Kelsey turned the gold ring on his finger. "You always forget that," she added.

"It just doesn't seem fair to you. You don't work for Tactec."

"Right. And you don't work for Bill Simon, but you have to deal when I work late," Kelsey replied. "We're here now because Bill wouldn't give me time off after our wedding. You're going to be understanding when my work gets in the way of our lives, and I'm going to do the same for you."

Tyler lifted Kelsey's hand and kissed it.

"Thank you," he said.

"Thank you for bringing me here," she said happily.

As the car drove up the E35 road, they talked about what they had seen and what they wanted to see. Both of them were looking forward to the museums and architecture that Florence had to offer. Kelsey had bought gifts for Morgan, Jasmine, her mom, and Grandma Rose, but she had some more shopping to do for Jess.

"So where's dinner this time?" Kelsey asked Tyler. She had a beautiful plum-colored dress packed for their special dinner in Florence.

"That's a surprise," Tyler said mischievously.

"It's always a surprise," Kelsey said. "Give me a hint. How many Michelin stars?"

"Zero," Tyler said.

"Then I don't want to eat there," Kelsey teased. She put a pout on her face, and Tyler laughed. They both knew that Kelsey couldn't care less whether a restaurant had a Michelin star. In fact, Kelsey was only barely aware of what one was.

"Oh, you're going to want to eat at the place I have planned for us this time. It's fit for a Princess. Even Princess Kelsey."

"We'll see," Kelsey said haughtily, and Tyler laughed again.

"You're a delight," he said, putting his arms around her and giving her a kiss. Kelsey sighed happily. It felt nice to be so loved.

The town car pulled up to a small building in the center of Florence.

"This is it," Tyler said to Kelsey.

"We're staying here?" Kelsey said, looking out of the window. It was nothing like their hotel had been in Rome.

"This is the place," Tyler said with a smile.

Kelsey looked at the building with a bit of surprise. It was like many of the buildings she had seen in Rome, beautiful and historic, but quite common for Italy. A small boutique selling children's clothes and a gelato store flanked a door marked only with a house number. But the biggest surprise was waiting inside.

"I can't believe this is our apartment," Kelsey said in awe, a few minutes later. They had just said goodbye to both Marco — who was returning with their driver to Rome — and their new butler, who had given them a tour of their new home.

"This is it," Tyler said, as he stood looking up at a tapestry that hung from the twenty-foot ceiling. It was just one of a number of stunning works of art that were around the apartment.

Their new home was an enormous luxury apartment, which it turned out was right in the heart of the city. Their butler, who would be available for them 24 hours a day, as he lived on-site, had called it the Palazzo Valenti, and Kelsey agreed, it was truly a palace.

In addition to the art, there were antiques everywhere. The four-bedroom, two-floor apartment had everything for a comfortable stay. Two dining rooms, a study, a modern kitchen and five elegant bathrooms, each decorated in the same Florentine style, made the apartment really feel like a home.

"This is amazing," Kelsey said, hugging Tyler, "Thank you."

"Actually, you can thank the media," Tyler said, giving Kelsey a kiss on the hair and nuzzling her. "We were supposed to stay in a hotel, but Conor thought that we would be overwhelmed by the paparazzi again if we stayed somewhere so high-profile again. We're a little more hidden here."

"I love this," Kelsey said. Not only was the apartment beautiful, it felt like a private home. "Let's cook dinner tonight." Kelsey looked up at Tyler. "Tonight's not the night you had planned for us to go to dinner, right?"

"No, we can cook," Tyler said. "Are you tired of Italian food? We could go out for something else."

Kelsey shook her head. "I just want to cook for you."

Tyler smiled at her. "This again?" he asked.

Kelsey pouted. "Stop making fun of me. Let me do nice things for you."

Tyler kissed her pouty lips. "You always do nice things for me, Princess," he replied.

A half-hour later, they had changed and were in a chic grocery store a few minutes walk from their apartment. Tyler picked up one of the small hand-held baskets.

"I was thinking about making risotto," Kelsey said. "But I think that might be a little boring, considering where we are."

"Anything's fine, Kels," Tyler said.

"I know, how about a frittata?"

"Sure."

"OK, so what do we need?" Kelsey thought. "Vegetables first," she decided.

"Over there," Tyler said. He took Kelsey's hand, and they headed for the vegetables. Kelsey saw a large zucchini, which she knew would be perfect for the frittata, so she picked it up and placed it into the basket. Next, she saw some big, bright-red tomatoes and just as she reached for one, someone shouted,

"*Basta!*"

Both Kelsey and Tyler turned. Standing next to them was a woman, who was frowning and shaking a pair of thin plastic gloves at Kelsey. The woman continued to talk angrily in Italian, while handing the gloves to Kelsey, who took them, confused.

Once the woman had said her piece, Tyler said, "*Scusi,*" to her. She gave him a nod and walked off, presumably to do her own shopping.

"What was that?" Kelsey asked.

"It seems that in Italy, when you pick up produce, you wear gloves so as not to get your germs on the vegetables," Tyler replied. It was clear that he was trying not to laugh.

"Are you kidding me?" Kelsey said.

Tyler shook his head. "No," he replied.

Kelsey looked down at the gloves in her hands.

"That's so wasteful," she said. "You're going to wash the vegetables at home anyway."

"True," Tyler agreed. "But that's the Italian way."

Kelsey sighed. "Fine," she said, putting on the gloves. She felt silly. Tyler turned and headed over to a metal tray which Kelsey noticed held even more plastic gloves. "Where are you going?"

"We're required to put the produce in plastic bags too," Tyler said, taking three of them from the dispenser.

Kelsey frowned, and Tyler gave her a grin.

"You wanted to come to the grocery store," he shrugged.

"Let's just do this, before we offend anyone else," Kelsey replied. Gloves on, she put the tomato in a plastic bag, and placed it into the basket.

Once Kelsey had finished selecting their vegetables, she followed Tyler over to a small scale.

"What are you doing?" she asked, as Tyler picked up one of the bags and placed it onto the scale. He pressed a button which had a picture of a tomato on it, and the scale printed out a small label.

"We have to price our own vegetables," Tyler said, putting the bag with the tomato back into the basket, and selecting another one.

Kelsey gave him a look.

"I didn't make the rules, Kelsey," Tyler commented.

"I'm starting to think we should have ordered out," Kelsey replied.

Hours later, the trip to the grocery store was forgotten, and the frittata had been consumed. Kelsey lay in Tyler's arms on the living room sofa of their palazzo, looking up at the ornate ceiling above them. Kelsey was sleepy as she snuggled against her husband.

"What are you thinking about?" she asked, stifling a yawn.

"You," Tyler replied. He leaned over and kissed her.

"What about me?" Kelsey asked.

"How you can be so calm about some things, and so worked up about others."

"What do you mean?"

"Tactec ruins two days of our honeymoon, and you don't blink an eye, but someone asks you to wear plastic gloves for two minutes, and you pout for a half-hour." Tyler replied.

"I didn't pout," Kelsey said with a smile. She had, and Tyler had noticed it earlier.

"OK," Tyler said. "You didn't pout. But why does one bother you, and the other doesn't?"

Kelsey thought as she stretched her bare legs out on the soft blanket below her. She cuddled a little closer to Tyler.

"It's taken me a while, but I'm starting to understand that I'm going to have to make some sacrifices to be with you," Kelsey began. "At first I was upset, because I hadn't really thought about how you being Lisa Olsen's son was going to affect me, and I felt overwhelmed. But I know

178

that you don't like it any more than I do, and we don't have a lot of control over what happens. There really isn't anyone to blame, it's just the way that things are. I know that you didn't want to go to the office, or to meet the mayor of Rome during your honeymoon, any more than I wanted you to do those things. It's the price that you have to pay because of who you are. I love who you are, and I wouldn't want you to be any other way. I also understand that there's no point in complaining about the situation that we're in sometimes."

Kelsey stroked Tyler's chest with her hand as she continued.

"Also, I actually don't mind doing most of the things that get thrown at us. It's not everyone who has the chance to meet the mayor of Rome on their honeymoon. I certainly didn't expect to when I was growing up in Port Townsend, Washington. There's a part of playing the role of Mrs. Tyler Olsen that's exciting, but mostly, I just love being your wife. And if that means that every few weeks I've got to make small talk with strangers, so be it. Because the rest of the time, I can talk to you."

Kelsey could see Tyler beam in the dim light. He held her close, and stroked her back with his hand.

"I don't know what I would do without you," Tyler said. "I'm so lucky to have you."

Kelsey smiled at him as she basked in his love.

"The feeling is mutual, Mr. Olsen," she said, and she gave him a kiss.

The next morning, Kelsey sat with Tyler on the small balcony of the apartment, overlooking the quiet Florence street. Tyler offered Kelsey a bite of toast with freshly-made strawberry jam, and she took it, licking the sweet jam off her lips. She watched as he glanced at her, then quickly looked away.

Kelsey smiled and rubbed Tyler's ankle with her toes under the stone table. He glanced at her happily, and his phone buzzed with a message. Both of them looked at it warily. Tyler picked it up and opened the message. He read for a moment, then he placed the phone in front of Kelsey so she could read it as well.

Kelsey looked down at the phone, and read the beginning of the message.

"No," she said firmly.

"This isn't one of the trials of being married to Tyler Olsen?"

"No. It's one of the trials of knowing Ryan Perkins," Kelsey replied.

"Scroll down. Ryan says she's lonely."

Kelsey took a very deep sigh.

"Fine," she conceded. "When does Ellie want to come?"

Kelsey couldn't help but feel grumpy as she got dressed a while later. Tyler had messaged Ellie, who seemed to be thrilled to leave her new home of Milan, Italy and take the train down to meet the couple in Florence. Ellie was married now, and of course, she and her husband had come to Port Townsend to see Tyler and Kelsey get married, although Kelsey had only seen them for the briefest of seconds. So there was no real reason to be upset, although she still was. However, at least she had two days to get used to the idea of dealing with Ellie again. Kelsey looked at herself in the mirror one more time, took another deep sigh, and left the bathroom.

Kelsey's mood changed the second she saw Tyler. He was lying on his back, on the bed, reading his Kindle. He looked over at Kelsey as she lay on the bed next to him.

"So what do you want to do for your birthday?" Kelsey asked. Tyler smiled wickedly, and Kelsey kissed him on the lips. "Besides that. I know you want to go the museums," she said.

"We should see David today." Tyler said, referring to the famous statue.

"That would be great," Kelsey said. She knew without asking that Jeffrey had arranged another private tour for them.

"I want to buy you a present," Tyler continued. Kelsey bit her lip. Tyler had bought Kelsey presents on his birthday before. Extravagant ones.

Tyler's brown eyes searched Kelsey's waiting for a response. She remained silent. Tyler smiled.

"And I want you to buy me a present," Tyler said.

"What do you want?" Kelsey asked.

"Whatever you think I would like," Tyler replied. Kelsey had an idea, and she felt herself blush at the thought of it.

"I have something in mind," she replied with a smile.

A few hours later, Kelsey and Tyler were walking down the Via de' Tornabuoni, holding hands. They had been to the Accademia Gallery, and as Kelsey had expected, they had a tour guide waiting for them. The David statue had been impressive, and it had been described by the tour guide as an example of male perfection. But in Kelsey's view, the embodiment of male perfection slept beside her every night.

Tyler kissed Kelsey's hand, and she smiled up at him. They had eaten lunch at a small trattoria that served amazing, rustic Tuscan food, and she was both full and happy. Now it was time to buy birthday presents, plus a few more things for Jess.

"Are you having a nice birthday, Tyler?" Kelsey asked.

"I'm having a wonderful birthday, Princess," Tyler replied.

"Who should we buy for first? Me, you, or Jess?"

"Me. I want to see what I'm getting for my birthday," Tyler replied. Kelsey felt herself blushing again. Tyler's birthday present would be a gift for both of them, and she got hot at the thought of it.

"OK," Kelsey said. "Let's stop for a minute." She pulled out her phone and typed into it. A lingerie shop was steps away, on the Via degli Strozzi. Kelsey noted the location, then put her phone into her jeans pocket. "Follow me," she said, pulling Tyler's hand.

A few minutes later, Tyler was sitting on a plush gold sofa, while a young woman was assisting Kelsey. Kelsey tried to avoid glancing over at Tyler because, since his phone had no internet, he had little to do but sit and watch her walk around the store. Kelsey found it distracting, because Tyler's quiet presence reminded her what the lingerie was for. For Tyler to remove from her body, slowly and seductively. Kelsey shook her head and tried to focus.

"*Signora* might like this one," the saleswoman said, holding up a black bodysuit, with elaborate white lace covering the front.

"*Signore* does," Tyler commented from the sofa. Kelsey gave him a look.

"You don't get a vote," she teased.

"It's my birthday present," Tyler replied with a pout.

Kelsey giggled. "Do you have it in red?" she asked the saleswoman.

"We do," the saleswoman replied brightly. "We also have a matching silk robe. Would you like to see it?"

"I would," Tyler piped up.

"Yes," Kelsey said to the saleswoman, ignoring Tyler.

Twenty minutes later, Kelsey had seen almost everything in the store, and a sizable pile of lingerie sat near the front counter waiting for her. Kelsey had seen the price of one item, and had almost left the store, but she reminded herself that not only could she now afford such things, but also they were for Tyler's birthday, and he would appreciate them. Kelsey took one final look around the store. Tyler was walking around, having grown tired of commenting from the sofa, and he had actually added two items to Kelsey's pile. A black see-through bodysuit was one item, and a sexy satin dress was the other. Kelsey wondered when she would wear the dress, as it was very form-fitting, but she thought that perhaps Tyler had a venue in mind. It didn't matter — since he had added it to the stack, she would buy it.

A saleswoman had joined Tyler as he looked on the other side of the shop. He pointed to a mannequin and said something to her. She nodded and walked off. Kelsey, curious about what Tyler had selected, walked over to him, her own saleswoman at her heels. Today would probably be a very good day for sales at the store.

Tyler's saleswoman returned just as Kelsey reached Tyler. She held a hanger in her hands. Tyler glanced at Kelsey.

"Will you wear that?" he asked Kelsey. She noted the sparkle in his eyes.

She smiled.

"For you I will," Kelsey replied.

Kelsey took deep, gasping breaths as Tyler kissed her neck. They had decided to postpone more shopping and instead, try out one of Kelsey's new purchases, a lacy red babydoll gown. It had worked as advertised, and now Kelsey was exhausted, and lay utterly relaxed in Tyler's strong arms. He nuzzled her ear. In the meantime, the lacy gown was in a soft heap on the carpeted floor.

Tyler was flushed as he kissed Kelsey on the lips.

"Happy birthday," Kelsey whispered.

Kelsey offered Tyler her hazelnut gelato cone a while later. She was refreshed after a short nap in Tyler's arms. He licked the cone seductively, and Kelsey giggled happily.

"Later," she said.

"Any time," Tyler replied with a wink.

Kelsey smiled at the thought. They had a lot of lingerie to get through, including Tyler's special request. But that particular piece would have to wait until their special dinner.

"Where to next?" Kelsey asked.

"I need to buy you a present," Tyler replied.

"You don't need to."

"I want to," Tyler said. Her first present, the diamond floral necklace, had been shipped back to Seattle.

"Can I get something more modest?" Kelsey asked hopefully.

"No," Tyler replied.

"I didn't think so," Kelsey said, under her breath.

"I have an idea," Tyler said. "Let's go buy the things on Jessica's list. That will put your gift in perspective."

Kelsey was sure that Tyler was correct about that. Florence was the home of two of Jessica's favorite designers, and she had requested that Kelsey stop by the flagship stores of both, to see if there were any exclusive items. If so, Kelsey was supoosed to purchase all of them, in every color.

On this trip, it was very easy for Kelsey to buy things for Jessica, thanks to the credit card that was in Kelsey's name but linked to Bob Perkins' account. Jessica had requested that Bob give Kelsey a card so Kelsey could more easily pick up things for Jess, and Bob had willingly done so. Already, Kelsey had spent several thousand dollars of Bob's money on items for Jessica, and today, she expected that she would spend quite a few more.

Kelsey realized that Tyler's plan had worked by the time they finished with the second store. She had spent thousands of dollars on just three items in the first store, and twice as much in the second. Her head was swimming at the expense, and at least once, her hand shook when she was signing the bill.

They were walking back across the Ponte Vecchio, a bridge that was lined with jewelry stores and souvenir shops. Tyler had led Kelsey across the bridge once, but they had turned around and headed back to the side of the river where they were staying without stopping at any stores.

Tyler held Kelsey's hand as they headed back through the city. It was still light, but the sun was slowly beginning to fade. Jessica's packages had been sent back to their apartment, and from there, would be shipped back to Medina, courtesy of Jeffrey, who was still on the Italian coast.

"You don't see anywhere you like?" Kelsey asked. They had passed many jewelry stores, and Kelsey was hoping that perhaps Tyler had decided that this birthday could pass without a gift for her.

"I'm taking you somewhere special," Tyler replied. "They're waiting for us."

"Oh," Kelsey said. She hadn't considered that Tyler might have a specific place in mind.

They walked slowly, stopping at the Fontana del Porcellino, making a small detour to stop at the Florence branch of Chanel, where they had a special shop devoted just to beauty products. Kelsey bought three lipsticks and a small travel makeup kit. After their surprise meeting with Rome's mayor, she thought that a makeup kit might be a good thing to pack in her suitcase from now on.

After a short stop at the Palazzo Vecchio, where they saw even more beautiful art, Tyler led Kelsey into a elegant jewelry store. As Tyler had said, the staff was waiting for the couple. They were greeted and escorted to a table, which had clearly been prepared for them.

"Mrs. Olsen," the salesman said in impeccable English once they were seated, "I understand that we will be making a one-of-a-kind piece for you."

Kelsey looked at Tyler, who said, "That's correct."

"Excellent," the salesman said pleasantly. "Did you have a specific idea in mind? A certain type of stone?"

"No," Kelsey managed to say.

"I'd like Kelsey to have something that will remind her of Florence," Tyler said.

The salesman beamed. "Lovely. We specialize in Florentine-style pieces, so I'm sure that we can make something that Mrs. Olsen will like. Will we be making a necklace or...?" the salesman asked, prompting Kelsey.

"Earrings," Kelsey said firmly. She had decided to put a limit on Tyler's generosity. Although there would be two of them, earrings would necessarily be relatively small. A handcrafted necklace could have dozens of jewels.

"Let me show you a few of our designs," the salesman said, "Then we can create something special for you."

Two hours later, Kelsey and Tyler arrived back at their apartment. They had placed the order with the jeweler, and in a couple of months, Kelsey would receive a pair of Florentine-style earrings, with three carats of diamonds in total. The jewelry store's artist had drawn a picture of a stunning pair of earrings, and to Kelsey's surprise, even though they were being handmade, they were half the price of the necklace that Tyler had bought for her in Rome.

Tyler placed Kelsey's Chanel store bag down on the coffee table, and sat on the sofa. Kelsey sat next to him, and leaned her head against his arm. It had been a busy day. Tyler put his arm around Kelsey's shoulders.

"We should go have dinner," he mused.

"We should," Kelsey agreed.

"Somewhere close," Tyler said.

"Why?" Kelsey asked.

"Because I want another birthday present," Tyler replied.

It was almost midnight by the time Kelsey had given Tyler his second birthday present, which this time had been wrapped up in the black bodysuit he had picked out in the lingerie store. Tyler licked chocolate frosting off Kelsey's finger as they sat in bed, eating the birthday cake which their butler had thoughtfully left in their room.

"Did you have a nice birthday?" Kelsey asked, as she wiped her hands with a tissue, hoping not to get frosting on the black silk robe she was now wearing.

"It was the best birthday ever," Tyler replied, his brown eyes sparkling.

"I'm glad that we got to spend it together," Kelsey said.

"Me too," Tyler replied, looking at her. Kelsey offered him another piece of cake, but Tyler shook his head.

"What?" Kelsey asked as Tyler continued to look at her.

"I just love you so much," Tyler said blissfully.

Kelsey leaned over and gave him a kiss.

"I love you too, Tyler," Kelsey replied, and she took a bite of cake.

The next morning, as sunlight streamed into the window, Kelsey woke up, enveloped in Tyler's arms. Her eyes fluttered, and a smile came to her lips. She loved being held by him, and instead of getting out of bed, Kelsey decided that she wanted to savor the moment for just a while longer.

An hour later, Kelsey was tying her running shoes, as Tyler surveyed her with his big brown eyes.

"Are you sure that you don't want me to go with you?" Tyler asked. Kelsey shook her head, and her ponytail gently hit her back.

"You can join me tomorrow," Kelsey replied. "We'll run through the streets of Florence together."

"Be safe," Tyler said as Kelsey leaned over onto the bed and kissed him.

"Back soon," Kelsey said, and she left the room.

Minutes later, Kelsey was running on the treadmill at the nearby gym that their butler had recommended. There was no particular hurry to get back, as Tyler had woken up to discover that he had a meeting with the head of Tactec Marketing to discuss his visit with the mayor of Rome.

Kelsey had been surprised, as it was past eleven p.m. on Friday in Seattle, but Tyler had noted that Jeffrey had told Marketing that it was the only time Tyler had available this week, in the hopes that they wouldn't bother the couple, but it hadn't worked.

When she returned to the apartment, Tyler was sitting on the sofa, showered and dressed. Kelsey was neither as she gave him a kiss.

"How was it?" she asked, pulling off her jacket.

"Tiresome," Tyler replied.

"You always say that."

"It's always true," Tyler said.

Kelsey thought as she removed her socks.

"You seem happy," she mused.

"What do you mean?" Tyler asked.

"I don't know. I just feel like this vacation has been good for you."

"You're good for me," Tyler replied.

Kelsey gave him a smile. "And you're good for me. I'm going to take my shower now."

"I could be better for you, if you invite me to join you," Tyler commented. Kelsey looked at him, and he looked back innocently.

"You're already clean," Kelsey said.

"I can get dirty," Tyler replied.

"You're serious? I thought we were going out," Kelsey said.

"Out is overrated. That's what my bride would say."

"Yes, she would," Kelsey agreed. She held out her hand, and pulled Tyler up from the sofa. "Come on, Mr. Olsen. Let's see how good you can be."

"What are you thinking about?" Tyler asked a while later. He stroked

Kelsey's hair, which was almost dry, thanks to the towel that she was lying on. After their shared shower, they had managed to make it to bed, but hadn't managed to completely dry off.

"I'm trying to figure out how I went from refusing to go to bed with you to being unable to get out of bed with you, in just three months," Kelsey replied.

"You got married?"

"I guess I didn't realize that getting married meant losing all of my inhibitions," Kelsey replied.

"Why would you have inhibitions with me?" Tyler asked curiously.

"I don't know. I just supposed that I would."

"I'm glad you don't," Tyler said, caressing her.

"Me too," Kelsey said happily.

"I love how you tell me what you want. It's very sexy."

"Is it?"

"It is," Tyler replied.

"You're very sexy, Mr. Olsen. That's why I'm always in bed with you," Kelsey said, cuddling against him. Tyler held Kelsey closer, and she closed her eyes happily.

A while later, Kelsey poked at the bowl in front of her with her fork, and looked at it doubtfully.

"What did you call this again?" she asked Tyler.

"*Panzanella.* Bread salad," he replied. He picked some up with his fork, and took a bite. "Try it. It's good."

Kelsey poked at the bowl again.

"This from the woman who can eat *lutefisk*," Tyler commented.

"This is kind of cold," Kelsey said, touching the bowl.

"Only the bowl is. The salad is at room temperature. Try it," Tyler said, holding some salad out on his fork and offering it to Kelsey. She opened her mouth reluctantly, but tasted it.

"It's not bad," Kelsey said, to her surprise. It hadn't seemed appetizing at first glance, a tomato-and-cucumber salad with too many large croutons, but Kelsey opened her mouth for another taste.

"Told you," Tyler said, giving her some more.

Kelsey chewed it and took a sip from her water glass.

"Know-it-all," she teased.

Tyler grinned. "I don't know everything."

"No?"

"No. Actually, I think I have a lot more to learn about you."

"I'm not sure that's true. You've known me for four years."

"I have, haven't I? Yet you're still a mystery to me," Tyler replied, eyes sparkling.

"I bet you've learned a few things on this vacation," Kelsey said seductively, and Tyler's smile got wider.

"A few," Tyler replied.

"OK, we're not having this conversation here," Kelsey said, because she was starting to blush.

"What conversation would you like to have, Princess?" Tyler asked, offering her another bite of *panzanella*.

"Tell me about your meeting," Kelsey said.

"That's certainly throwing cold water on things," Tyler replied.

"Sorry, but you haven't told me any details, and I know that you're thinking about it," Kelsey replied. Tyler hadn't mentioned it to her on the walk to the restaurant, but instead he had been quiet.

"The meeting was fine, they just wanted to make sure that I hadn't made any promises to the mayor."

"Then what were you thinking about?" Kelsey asked.

"Us," Tyler replied.

"What about us?"

"I was thinking about what you said. That I seemed happy on this vacation. And I am, and I hope that you are too."

"I am," Kelsey beamed.

"I'm just trying to figure out how to make that last. I know how easy it's going to be to get caught up in work again when we get back, and I want things to be different."

Kelsey nodded. She understood too. Life in Seattle had been a whirlwind for both of them.

"I don't want our time to only be on the weekends when we don't have things to do. I want us to have time together during the day."

"How is that possible?" Kelsey said, and she felt a shiver. *Was Tyler going to ask her to quit her job?*

"Maybe it isn't," Tyler said. "I don't know. I could have go have lunch with you at Simon's office sometimes. Or use my flextime more wisely."

Kelsey breathed a mental sigh of relief.

"I just want more Kelsey time," Tyler said. "And if I don't figure out how to carve it out of my day soon, I'll be like Lisa when I'm CEO."

"Lisa sees her boyfriends," Kelsey said, choosing not to mention Lisa's current boyfriend's name.

"Not as much as I want to see you," Tyler replied. "I've really missed having time like this with you."

"Me too," Kelsey agreed. She had loved her last long weekend with Tyler in Tacoma, but being in Italy reminded her of vacations in law school, when they had time to just hang out and be together for days on end. "It's hard to balance the responsibilities of being grown up," she added.

"But we both need to," Tyler replied.

Kelsey bit her lip. Tyler was right. Although she loved her job, she did occasionally need to place it second, after her marriage. She had been reluctant to do so in the past, partly because she felt that Tyler wasn't willing to make sacrifices for her. But she had been wrong.

"We do," she agreed.

They spent their Saturday unhurriedly walking south of the Arno river. They spent two hours in the Palazzo Pitti, looking at the vast art collection, then after a pasta lunch, they walked through the Boboli Gardens. Kelsey loved the nature, even though the gardens were laid out quite formally.

"Do you know people who live like this?" Kelsey asked as they walked. The garden had once been the private property of the Medici family, and had only been for their use.

"A few," Tyler said. "Actually, so do you. Ellie doesn't live in the city of Milan, she lives in the countryside outside of the city at the Palazzo Librizzi."

Kelsey looked at Tyler in wonder. 'Palazzo' meant palace in Italian, and Kelsey had been in quite a few during their trip.

"Ellie lives in a palace?" she said.

"I think so. It's been in the Librizzi family for centuries," Tyler said. "I doubt it's this big, though."

"Wow," Kelsey said.

"Would you like to live in a palace?" Tyler asked curiously.

"No. I think I'm a city girl," Kelsey replied.

"If you change your mind, let me know," Tyler said.

"Why? Would you buy me a palace?" Kelsey asked.

"If you'd like," Tyler replied.

"Show-off," Kelsey teased.

"A palace outside of Milan is probably cheaper than a shoebox in the city of Seattle," Tyler noted. Kelsey had to agree. House prices in Seattle were astronomical, thanks to the numerous tech companies headquartered there. She suspected that even Tyler hesitated to invest in Seattle real estate these days, thanks to the cost.

"Our home in Seattle is fine," Kelsey said. "I don't need a palace."

"Every princess needs a palace," Tyler said.

"No, every princess needs a Prince Charming," Kelsey replied. "And I have mine."

The next morning, Kelsey and Tyler got up early to go running. Unlike the day before when Kelsey had run in the gym, they ran through the quiet streets of Florence. It was Sunday, and most Italians were still tucked in bed or having breakfast, as Kelsey and Tyler raced through the streets, happily chasing each other.

Kelsey needed to run today and de-stress a little, because later they would join the former Ellie Grant, now Countess Eleanor Librizzi, for lunch. Kelsey expected that spending time with Ellie would not be relaxing at all.

Heads turned as Ellie walked to their table at lunch. As always, Ellie looked stunning, but today she looked even more so, as she was wearing a beautiful sweater dress in the colors of fall, with gold flecks in the yarn. Kelsey felt a little underdressed in her jeans and sneakers, but after all, she was on vacation.

"Hi," Ellie said happily as the couple stood to greet her. She gave both of them air kisses in the Italian way, both cheeks. They all sat down, although Ellie sat a little less gracefully than Kelsey would have expected, based on her dress. It was more of a plop.

"How is the *Contessa*?" Tyler asked Ellie.

She gave him a dark look. "I'm sure you know how I am. How's Vic?"

"Fine," Tyler replied. "Thanks for coming down to see us," he said.

"I wouldn't have known you were here if I hadn't seen you in the news," Ellie said, and Kelsey saw the beginnings of Ellie's signature pout.

"We didn't want to get in the way. We didn't have plans to go to Milan," Tyler said, and Kelsey thought he sounded sincere.

"You should have come up. I would have shown you around. I have nothing else to do," Ellie sighed.

"You aren't your usual self," Tyler said. "How are you?"

"Bored," Ellie replied. "Didn't Ryan tell you?"

"He said that he thought you needed to see a friendly face," Tyler replied.

"That's why he sent Kelsey," Ellie said, smiling at her.

Tyler laughed. "I can leave."

"No, I'm just grumpy. It's nice to see you too."

"Why are you bored?" Tyler asked.

"Nothing to do," Ellie repeated.

"You could work. You live in the fashion capital of Italy. I'm sure lots of people would love an American fit model."

"Tyler, Countess Librizzi could not possibly work outside of the house. That would bring shame upon the Librizzi name," Ellie said, and Kelsey could hear the irritation in her voice.

"Then what are you doing?" Kelsey asked curiously.

Ellie looked thoughtful. "I got my nails done yesterday," she concluded.

"You have nothing to do?" Tyler asked.

Ellie brushed a strand of her hair back. "Let's order," she said, picking up her menu. "Then I'll tell you my story."

Orders placed, Ellie continued. Kelsey was very curious about what she was going to say, because the bright, outgoing Ellie whom she had met ages ago seemed to be very different from the young woman who was sitting at their table now. Ellie absentmindedly twisted her hair as she spoke.

"Matteo became the head of his family's textile business when his father died. That's why he was in New York, to drum up business. The company is doing really well now, but Matteo works twenty hours a day. His two sisters and his mother rely on him, so he takes his responsibilities very seriously," Ellie said, and from her tone, Kelsey could tell that Ellie really admired this about Matteo.

"But because of the family name, Matteo doesn't want me working, not even in the company. All of our money goes back into the business, so it's not like I can spend my days shopping. And as it is, Matteo's sisters and I usually wear the samples from the designers that we supply textiles to, like what I'm wearing now," she said, pointing to her dress. "We get them for free, and we're walking advertisements for the company."

"Kimmy said I should have a baby," Ellie went on, "And that would certainly give me something to do. But Matteo doesn't want children. Jess told me I should learn to knit, and I did that. I made a cashmere sweater for Matteo." Ellie thought for a moment. "I take Italian lessons, and I'm pretty bad at them. Ryan suggested that I learn to cook, but my mother-in-law won't hear of someone cooking for her son other than herself. I read, go to the gym, and pray that Matteo takes me on his next business trip to New York, but he never does."

Tyler looked at Ellie in disbelief. Kelsey understood why. Kelsey would have never given in the way that Ellie seemed to have in her relationship.

"So during the week I spend my days trying to think of things to do. On Saturdays, Matteo usually takes me out, and on Sundays we go to Mass and at dinner afterwards I listen to his aunts cluck about why I'm not pregnant yet," Ellie concluded. "So that's my life."

"You could change it," Tyler replied.

"I love Matteo, so no, I can't," Ellie replied.

"I'm sorry," Tyler said.

Ellie nodded. "You two seem to be happy," she commented. Tyler glanced at Kelsey.

"We are," Kelsey replied for the two of them. Tyler beamed.

"Why didn't you go on your honeymoon sooner?" Ellie asked, picking up her glass of wine that the waiter had unobtrusively left while she had been speaking.

"Kelsey couldn't get time off," Tyler replied.

"You're still working?" Ellie said in disbelief. "You're married to Tyler. He wouldn't let you sit at home alone."

"I like working," Kelsey said.

"Jessica said the same thing to me," Ellie said. "Ryan's not going back to work now that the kids are here, so I don't understand why she is."

"What do you wish you were doing?" Tyler asked Ellie. Kelsey sensed that he felt bad about the situation that Ellie was in.

Ellie sighed, and Kelsey thought that she saw her eyes get a little misty. "I just wish I didn't feel so useless," she said.

"You could work online," Tyler prodded. Ellie shook her head.

"I'm not smart like Vic. I don't know what I could do." She twisted her hair some more. "Matteo says that once the company is a little more stable, he'll have more time for me. So I'll wait until he does, and fill in my days as I can."

"Are you sure?" Tyler asked.

"Is Tyler Olsen actually concerned about me?" Ellie asked.

"Of course I am. You're my friend," Tyler replied. Ellie reached out and stroked his hand with her own beautifully-manicured one.

"Thank you, Tyler. I'll be OK," Ellie replied.

Ellie and Kelsey stood outside the restaurant while Tyler was paying the bill inside. The two of them were attracting quite a bit of unwanted male attention from passers-by on the street, but they ignored it.

"Tyler seems very happy," Ellie commented to Kelsey.

"I hope so," Kelsey replied.

"I've seen a lot of sides of Tyler Olsen," Ellie continued. "But happy is one I've only seen since you came into his life," she said. "I'm glad you did."

"Thanks, Ellie," Kelsey replied sincerely.

Tyler came out of the restaurant and joined them.

"Are you heading back to Milan?" Tyler asked Ellie. "Do you want us to walk you back to the train station?"

Ellie shook her head. "No, go and enjoy the rest of your honeymoon. I'll head back in a bit, I'm going to make the most out of being in Florence." Ellie gave Kelsey two air kisses.

"We're always here if you need us," Tyler said, and Kelsey could hear the message that Tyler was sending to Ellie. Unlike some women, Ellie was not stuck in her situation. "If you decide that you want to come back, just let me or Ryan know, and we'll take care of you."

"I know," Ellie said. "Ryan said that Bob would send his plane for me."
She smiled. "I'll let you know," she said.

"Any time," Tyler said, as Ellie air-kissed his cheeks again. "Day or
night."

"Thank you, Tyler. I'll be OK," Ellie repeated. "Take care of yourselves,"
she said to the couple.

"You too, Ellie," Kelsey said. And with a wave, Ellie walked off.

Tyler took Kelsey's hand, and they headed in the opposite direction.

"That was depressing," Tyler editorialized. "Why is she staying?"

"I guess she loves him," Kelsey said.

"But how can he love her if he's letting her be so miserable?" Tyler
asked.

"Maybe he doesn't know. Ellie said that he works all the time," Kelsey
replied.

"He should know how she's feeling if he loves her," Tyler replied. Then,
without warning, Tyler stopped walking and looked at Kelsey. "Are you
unhappy?" he asked.

"No," Kelsey replied with a smile.

"I'm not missing anything?"

"Of course not," Kelsey said.

"You're happy?"

"Ecstatic."

"Good," Tyler said, resuming their walk. "Then I can judge Matteo."

Kelsey laughed. "What do you want to do?" she asked.

"I don't know what I can do," Tyler replied. "If Ellie wants to stay, that's her choice."

"At least she knows she doesn't have to," Kelsey said comfortingly. "I think she was happy to hear that from you."

"I hope so," Tyler mused.

"You really care about her, don't you?"

"Ellie is a thorn in my side," Tyler replied.

"I know, but she's like your little sister."

"Maybe," Tyler conceded.

"Ellie will let you know if she needs something," Kelsey said.

But Tyler shook his head. "She's not like you," he replied. "I can't be sure of her telling me if something's really wrong."

"How about Ryan? Will she tell him?"

"No. Maybe Kim, though. I'll tell Ryan to have Kim check in with her occasionally."

"I'm sure that Ellie would appreciate that," Kelsey replied.

Tyler surveyed Kelsey. "Thanks for not being jealous," he commented.

"It's fine. I have male friends."

"Yes, but I'm jealous of them," Tyler replied.

Kelsey giggled and hugged Tyler's arm. "You have no reason to be. I'm yours," she replied.

On Monday night, Kelsey was getting dressed in one of the large bathrooms in their Florence apartment. And she was struggling.

Tonight she would wear the special piece of lingerie that Tyler had asked her to buy, but despite the help of the internet, it was still taking her a while to put it on. It turned out that garter belts could be a little tricky.

The bra and panties of course, had been a breeze to put on. And the garter belt itself wasn't difficult once Kelsey figured out how to open the clasps. The difficulty lay in attaching the thigh-high stocking to the garter belt and not having the silky stocking slip away. It was taking more time than Kelsey expected.

She sat on the padded bench in the bathroom and took a deep breath. Gravity was working against her, so she would start again. She lifted the thigh-high stocking by the lace top, very carefully, so as not to get a run. Kelsey smoothed it against her thigh, then gently took the back snap of the garter belt and attached the stocking to it. She breathed a sigh of relief when she tugged at it and realized it was firmly in place. She snapped the front snap to the front of the stocking, smoothed the stocking once more, and felt a sense of accomplishment. Lingerie was more complex than she had realized.

She put on the other stocking, attached it to the garter belt, then stood up and looked in the mirror. The garter belt set was beautiful. It was a stunning peacock blue, with ribbons and lace. Kelsey had to admit that she looked pretty good in it. She was sure Tyler would think so.

Kelsey turned back to the rest of her wardrobe for the evening. A plum silk dress was hung up on the back of the bathroom door, and underneath were plum satin shoes. The shoes were beautiful low heels and Kelsey was surprised to find that they were quite comfortable. She supposed that Jeffrey knew something about her destination that she didn't. Otherwise, Kelsey was quite confident that he would have packed a high heel for her. He seemed to prefer them when dressing her.

Kelsey was very curious as to what Tyler had planned for her. It was Monday, and once again, all of the museums had been closed, so they had spent the day shopping for Jess, eating gelato, and visiting as many outdoor historical sites as they could find. They would take the train from Florence to Venice tomorrow afternoon. They hadn't been to the world famous Uffizi Gallery yet, so Kelsey expected that they would go before their train tomorrow, since it had been closed today. She couldn't imagine that Tyler would want to miss it.

Kelsey pulled on the plum dress, and adjusted the peacock blue bra strap so it wouldn't be seen. She took a look in the mirror, brushed her long blonde hair behind her ear, and glanced at the sparkle of the gold earrings that swung with her movement. She was ready to go.

Tyler was standing in the living room, waiting for her. Once again, he was wearing a perfectly-tailored suit, and as always, he looked delectable in it. His brown eyes took her in as she stepped out into the room.

"You look amazing," Tyler said, coming to her side, and kissing her. "So beautiful."

"Thank you," Kelsey said, looking up at him. "You look nice too."

"Thanks. Are you ready to go?" he asked.

"When you are," Kelsey replied.

She picked up her clutch, and Tyler helped her drape a cream-colored cashmere wrap around her shoulders. He took her hand, and they slowly walked out to their waiting town car.

Tyler sat away from her in the car, and instead of being insulted, Kelsey was delighted. She knew that Tyler thought that she looked irresistible, but he didn't want to ruin her makeup or wrinkle her clothes with his affections. There would be time for that later, but for now, they had somewhere to go.

The town car drove through the streets of Florence, and Kelsey saw many of the sights that they had seen on their walks over the past few days. Palazzos and piazzas glowed in the slowly setting sun. Kelsey was surprised that they were leaving for dinner so early, but she suspected that Tyler had a surprise waiting for her before they ate. Kelsey was trying to be patient, because she knew that she didn't have long before she found out.

Tyler held her hand, and the gold bangle that hung from Kelsey's right wrist rested against his pant leg. He did not speak, but looked out of the window on his own side of the car. A few moments later the town car stopped, and Tyler helped Kelsey out of the car. They were standing in the Piazza della Signoria, where they had been several times before. The town car drove away, and Tyler looked at Kelsey.

"Let's walk," he said.

Kelsey held Tyler's hand and was happy for her warm wrap — Italy was becoming cooler as September progressed. They walked by some of the statues they had seen before, and paused to look closer at some of the statues in the night. There were many tourists around them, who paid the couple no mind.

"It's beautiful here," Kelsey said to Tyler. "Thank you for bringing me."

"Thank you for suggesting Italy," Tyler replied, as he gave her hand a kiss.

"Where would you have taken me if I hadn't?" Kelsey asked curiously.

"Back to Kalaloch," Tyler teased.

"You would not have," Kelsey pouted.

"I don't know. Maybe here," Tyler admitted. Kelsey smiled and they walked on.

They walked through a corridor of statues that Kelsey didn't recognize. They represented some of the men who had put Florence on the map. Michelangelo, Botticelli and many more were there, looking down on the tourists that looked up to them.

Kelsey wondered where they were headed, because instead of walking towards an area with restaurants, they seemed to be walking further away from the city.

"Where are we going?" Kelsey asked, her curiosity getting the best of her.

"The Uffizi Gallery," Tyler replied.

"It's closed."

"Not for us, it isn't," Tyler replied with a grin.

Less than five minutes later, Kelsey stood in the Uffizi Gallery, with Tyler and the director of the gallery at her side. She was awestruck. It wasn't just that she was standing in one of the most famous places in the art world, but she had just discovered that for tonight, it was reserved just for her.

Kelsey and Tyler wandered the Uffizi Gallery for hours, an English-speaking tour guide at their side. Kelsey had never been to a museum like this — every room empty of visitors, but full of art. They held hands and stopped at every piece of art that interested them. Tyler was knowledgeable about many of the pieces, and Kelsey loved learning about the art in front of her. They stood in front of many of the most famous pieces for a long time, including the Birth of Venus by Botticelli and Doni Tondo by Michelangelo.

"Are you hungry?" Tyler asked after a while.

"I am," Kelsey admitted. "But I don't want to leave."

Tyler gave her a smile. "We don't have to," he said.

Kelsey sat down at a elegant table for two. She was almost shaking in surprise. The table was in one of the corridors of the Uffizi, and they were surrounded by art. As the server walked away from the table, Kelsey leaned over to Tyler.

"I'm in shock," she admitted.

"Is that a good or bad thing?"

"Good. Tyler, how did you arrange this?' Tyler said nothing, but smiled at her instead. The string quartet Tyler had hired to play music for them while they dined began, and classical music filled the air. Kelsey looked disbelievingly at her husband, who took her hands gently into his own and kissed her fingertips.

"Thank you for marrying me," Tyler said simply, and he kissed her ring finger.

It was almost midnight by the time they arrived back at their apartment. The night had been magical, and Kelsey knew by the way that Tyler kissed her that he had more magic planned for her.

She walked into the bedroom — plum dress off — but bra, panties and garter belt on. Tyler, who was laying on the bed waiting for her, surveyed Kelsey with his eyes.

"Wow," he said.

"Do you like it?" Kelsey asked softly. She felt a little shy. She had worn many types of lingerie in front of Tyler before, but this was very new. Something about it shouted 'sex' to her.

Tyler continued to look at her.

"I love you," he replied. He stood up, ran his finger under Kelsey's bra strap, and kissed her shoulder. Kelsey felt her breathing get faster.

Tyler's hands slowly caressed her waist and slid to her thighs. He kissed her as his hand reached back up and undid her bra. He tugged it gently, and Kelsey let it fall to the ground.

Kelsey watched as Tyler knelt before her. He smiled as he fingered the clasp of the garter belt, and with a sharp snap, opened it. Obviously, garter belts were not new to Tyler. A moment later, he had opened the second clasp, and Kelsey felt the silky stocking fall to the ground. As Tyler reached out for the other side of the garter belt, Kelsey closed her eyes in anticipation.

It was time for more of Tyler's magic.

"You liked Florence, Princess?" Tyler asked her on the train the next morning.

"I loved Florence," Kelsey said. Her head was leaning on Tyler's

211

shoulder, both of her hands in his.

"Me too," Tyler replied. "Sorry about this morning."

Lisa had called him to discuss a board matter that would affect the company in the long term. It was clear to Kelsey that Lisa fully intended for Tyler to be CEO sooner rather than later.

"Tyler, it's fine."

"No, it's not. I'm done picking up the phone," Tyler said.

Kelsey giggled. "You don't have to do that," she said.

"I want to spend time with you. Not on the phone dealing with Tactec."

"We're going back to Rome in less than a week. Maybe you'll be dealing with Tactec in person," Kelsey teased.

"No way. Anyway, we're switching hotels. The paparazzi won't find us this time. And like I said, I'm done picking up the phone."

Kelsey nuzzled him, and Tyler kissed her hair.

"I don't mind. I know that I have to share you with Tactec," Kelsey said.

"Not now you don't. This is our time together," Tyler said firmly.

"OK, Mr. Olsen," Kelsey said happily. "Don't answer your phone."

"I won't," Tyler said as the train began to move. "Look outside," he said. "We'll be going too fast in a few minutes for you to see anything." Kelsey looked out the window, and Tyler kissed her hair again.

As Tyler had predicted, the train sped across the countryside to their new destination, Venice. The couple barely had time to watch a movie together and eat the paninis that they had bought on the way to the station before they were in the town car waiting for them at the Venice train station.

"You don't think that having your luggage flown across the country is extravagant?" Kelsey asked Tyler a while later, as she opened the curtains of their suite a little wider, so they could have a better view of the Grand Canal.

"Of course it is," Tyler said. "But I didn't want to drag our luggage on the train, and trains don't have baggage service."

Kelsey glanced at him, and Tyler shrugged.

"Fine," she said. The expense of having two pieces of luggage flown to Venice was clearly nothing compared to the cost of the room she was standing in.

"Don't worry. When we're back in Seattle, the biggest extravagance I'll have is a Starbucks coffee," Tyler said.

Kelsey laughed. "Not true. I've seen our new house."

"Have to live somewhere," Tyler replied. He reached out his arms, and Kelsey walked over to him and sat in his lap. Tyler put his arms around her and closed his eyes.

"Are you tired?" Kelsey asked. They had been up very late, and had got up early to enjoy their last few moments in Florence.

"No. Just happy," Tyler replied.

The couple walked to the Rialto Bridge, then had an early dinner at at Venice restaurant which boasted that it had been open for over 500 years.

They shared *cicchetti*, small plates of delicious food.

"It's Venice's version of tapas," Kelsey commented, offering Tyler half a meatball.

"Speaking of Spain, how's Miss Hill?" Tyler asked.

"Worried about going back to work?" Kelsey asked.

"Lisa said I'll be back in Bob's office when I get back, so I'm kind of wondering what mood he's going to be in."

Kelsey picked up her phone and looked at Instagram. Morgan had been posting every day, but Kelsey noticed that something had changed.

"The last thing she posted was on Saturday," Kelsey commented. As it was now Tuesday in the United States, that was notable. "She was working. A boy's birthday party."

"Morgan works on children's birthday parties?" Tyler asked.

"Morgan works on any party that someone can afford to pay her firm for," Kelsey said wisely. "Anyway this wasn't just any party. I saw a climbing wall with a giant bow in the background."

"Really?" Tyler said in amusement. "How old is he?" Kelsey looked down at the post.

"Seven," she said.

"Divorced parents who work in tech, are super busy, and feel guilty about not spending time with him," Tyler said.

"How can you know that?" Kelsey asked.

"I got my climbing wall when I was eight," Tyler replied.

Tyler had arranged another surprise for Kelsey when they returned to the hotel. She went to the luxurious hotel spa for a massage while Tyler remained in their room. Jeffrey had sent over Tyler's financial accounting for the month of August over a week ago, and Tyler had been postponing reviewing it.

Kelsey lay on the table as the scent of rose drifted through the air. She breathed in the floral scent as the masseur gently kneaded her back muscles. As she lay in the warm room, Kelsey knew that there would be little for the masseur to do today, because all of Kelsey's tension had melted away during her honeymoon with Tyler. The only problem from Kelsey's perspective was that they had reached the halfway point of their vacation, and in just a week and a half they would find themselves back in the real world.

Tyler was talking on the phone as Kelsey walked back into their suite an hour later. He gave her a wink as he spoke into the phone to someone.

"I knew that September would be an expensive month for us. It's fine."

Tyler paused to listen, but he gestured for Kelsey to join him on the sofa. She did so, and leaned her head on Tyler's chest.

"No, I appreciate your concern, David. Especially with Jeffrey."

Tyler laughed, Kelsey supposed, at the comment from the person on the other end of the line.

"Yeah, I completely agree. I'll be going through his expense account with a fine-tooth comb. After what he pulled with Lisa for my wedding, I'm probably going to make him give me the receipts."

There was another pause, then Tyler said,

"Yes, Camille's fine. There's going to be a lot of expenses because the place on Western is a complete shell. She'll stick to the budget, but knowing Camille, she'll probably have a surplus at the end."

At the mention of their new condo, Kelsey felt a little funny. She twisted the soft terry-cloth belt of the robe she was wearing.

"That would be great. I'd appreciate getting the report earlier in the month so I can deal with Jeffrey sooner in the month of October than later. Thanks. OK, I'll talk to you when we get back."

Tyler laughed again.

"Thanks, David. Bye."

Tyler hung up the phone and put his arms around Kelsey.

"You smell great. Did you have fun?" he asked.

"It was really nice, Tyler. Thank you," Kelsey said softly. Tyler looked at her curiously.

"Did you want to say something, Mrs. Olsen?"

"Who were you talking to?"

"David Sheinman," Tyler replied.

Kelsey bit her lip. That was who she had assumed. Tyler's financial advisor.

Kelsey took a deep sigh, then she turned her body to be able to look directly at Tyler.

"Tyler, I don't want you spending all of your money on me," she said.

"I can't possibly spend all of my money on you," Tyler replied.

"Tyler, you know what I mean."

"Don't worry about money, Princess," Tyler said breezily. He slipped a finger into the opening of Kelsey's terry-cloth robe and peeked inside at her bra. "I'm enjoying everything that I buy for you as much as you are. Maybe more."

"I know, but while we're here, you're renovating the new condo too."

"It's fine, I can afford it."

"It doesn't need to be fancy though," Kelsey said.

"It won't be."

"I know that Camille was in charge of renovating Ryan and Jess's house, and that cost a lot."

"I have to live there too. We aren't sleeping in a tent on the bare floor," Tyler commented.

Kelsey giggled. She tossed her hair back. "That might be fun, though." she replied.

Tyler looked at Kelsey with his sexy brown eyes.

"Let me spend some of my money on you. On us. No complaints," he said, brushing a strand of Kelsey's hair back. She put her finger on his lips and he kissed it.

"No complaints. Thank you," Kelsey conceded.

"You're welcome," Tyler replied. He reached out and undid the belt of Kelsey's robe, which fell open. "I have a completely free activity that I'd like to do with you." he said. Kelsey smiled.

"Gee, I wonder what that would be," she asked as Tyler pulled the terry-cloth robe down off her shoulder.

"One guess," Tyler said, kissing her neck.

Unlike Rome and Florence, in Venice Kelsey knew that they would be staying in two different hotels, in two different locations on the Grand Canal. So for their first full day in the city, the couple spent the day visiting the attractions on their hotel's side of the Grand Canal. They walked through the natural history museum, had lunch in a tiny cafe in the Campo San Polo, and saw more incredible art in the Basilica dei Frari.

They ended up in Cannaregio, one of the less touristy areas of Venice, as the sun was setting.

"We're lost again," Kelsey said delightedly. They had lost their bearings at least a dozen times in the tiny historic streets.

"At least we won't starve. We passed about a dozen restaurants in the past five minutes," Tyler commented.

"Are you hungry?"

"For you," Tyler replied seductively.

"Too bad, because we have no idea where we are."

"I know where you are. That's all that matters," Tyler said, putting his arm around her waist.

On Thursday, Kelsey and Tyler left their hotel to do the tourist circuit of Venice while their things were moved to their second hotel. They rode in a gondola, took pictures in St. Mark's Square, and bought postcards and pasta in the shape of carnival hats. Around three p.m., they headed for their hotel for the next few nights. As they entered the hotel from the land entrance, Kelsey looked around in awe.

"I know why they call this a palace," she commented.

They were greeted like long-lost family by the hotel manager, which Kelsey knew to mean that once again Tyler had rented an expensive suite for them. And once they arrived, Kelsey wasn't surprised to see a beautiful suite, with another beautiful view. But there was something interesting about this particular suite.

"Why is there a staircase?" she asked Tyler.

"Maybe you should go look," Tyler replied innocently. Kelsey searched Tyler's brown eyes with her own, but read nothing but amusement there.

"Fine. I will," she replied. And she headed up the circular stairs.

Kelsey's eyes widened as she reached the top. She covered her mouth with her hand in surprise.

"Tyler," she whispered.

A few minutes later, Tyler had joined her on their private, two-level terrace overlooking the Grand Canal. Santa Maria Salute Church was in full view as they sat on the edge of the private pool.

"I will never forget this view," Kelsey said to Tyler.

"It's beautiful," Tyler agreed.

Kelsey looked at him, but she was at a loss for words, so she turned back to the view of the Grand Canal. Tyler gently stroked her hand as Kelsey sat, her mind trying to comprehend everything she had seen and done over the past two weeks.

Tyler was so kind and so generous, and he always had been, from the moment that he had become a part of Kelsey's life. And now, as Mrs. Tyler Olsen, Kelsey was experiencing things that she had barely realized were possible. She loved being with Tyler, and a part of her knew that being with Tyler meant that these types of experiences would be the new normal for her. It was nothing for Tyler to spend ten thousand dollars on a hotel suite. The difficulty for him would be having the time off to enjoy it with Kelsey.

It was hard for Kelsey to understand this, because money had almost always been the limiting factor in her life, not time. In Port Townsend, she had nothing but time, and it had taken her a lot of work to learn how to use it wisely. Time had slowly become more limited as she had gone through school, and now working for Simon, she sort of understood why time was so precious to Tyler.

However, she still didn't understand quite how Tyler related to money. Every expense was the same to him, from a one-Euro cone of gelato, to thousands of Euros to buy a necklace that Kelsey would wear a few times a year. As she sat overlooking Venice's Grand Canal, holding her husband's hand, Kelsey wondered if she ever would understand him, and perhaps more importantly, if it mattered if she ever did.

Kelsey watched as Tyler's eyes opened the next morning. She was surrounded by his strong arms, and had been all night. Thousands of Euros' worth of lingerie was in a heap by the side of the luxurious bed, which was one of the many reasons that Kelsey had spent much of the night not sleeping, but looking at the opulent ceiling instead.

"Hey, beautiful," Tyler said sleepily, giving Kelsey a kiss. "Have you been awake long?"

"A while," Kelsey admitted. Tyler reached his hand up and rubbed his eyes.

"Do you feel OK?" he asked. "You were kind of quiet last night."

"Why do you always think something's wrong when I'm quiet?" Kelsey teased.

"I'm thinking that you know the answer to that question," Tyler replied.

"I'm OK," Kelsey said. "I'm just struggling with your lifestyle again," she admitted.

"You really need to get with the program," Tyler commented.

"I'm trying. I really am," Kelsey said. "But I grew up in a family where having a bed, instead of a sleeping bag, on vacation was an unbelievable luxury."

"I know," Tyler said sympathetically.

"It's not that I don't appreciate all of this," Kelsey said hurriedly, "I do. I'm just not used to it."

"I want you to get used to it," Tyler replied.

"I know you do," Kelsey said.

"Just keep trying. Soon you'll be like Jess."

221

"I'll never be like Jess," Kelsey said. "No matter how much I try."

"Let me spoil you for one more week," Tyler said. "Then you can go back home and be Kelsey Olsen, intellectual property lawyer again."

"In her gigantic home overlooking Elliott Bay," Kelsey added.

Tyler frowned. "I told you to get with the program," he said firmly.

Kelsey giggled at his petulant look. "Yes, Mr. Olsen," she said in mock obedience.

"Are you at least having fun?" Tyler asked.

"I have never had a better time in my life," Kelsey admitted. "But it's because I'm with you, not because of everything we're surrounded by."

Tyler smiled at her. "I'm glad. I wish we always had this much time together."

"Me, too," Kelsey admitted.

"But you have a career, and I'm going to be CEO, so we'll have to enjoy each other's company when we can."

"That's why we're doing all of this, right? Because we won't have time later?"

"I want every second I have with you to be memorable, so you won't forget me when I'm gone," Tyler replied.

"Tyler, you're exaggerating. I'll see you at home every night," Kelsey said.

Tyler pulled her closer. "I just want you to be happy," he said softly.

"Things don't make me happy. Being with you makes me happy," Kelsey said.

"But I can't give that to you. You know that," Tyler replied.

Kelsey stroked his arm. "You'll give me the time that you have, and I will love every minute of it," Kelsey said. "You never have to think that I don't know that you love me."

"Ellie made me think," Tyler admitted. "She's a bird in a gilded cage, and her husband probably has no idea how much she's hurting."

"You are not Matteo, and I am certainly not Ellie," Kelsey said. "I will let you know if I'm not OK."

"You promise?"

"I did today," Kelsey reminded him.

"OK," Tyler said. He stroked her hair and kissed her lips. His brown eyes searched hers for a moment, then he pulled her even closer. "You are my world, Kelsey Anne. Never forget that."

"I won't," Kelsey said, closing her eyes peacefully, enveloped in Tyler's arms.

After a full day during which they visited the many museums and historic churches near their hotel, they returned to their suite to get dressed for dinner. Once again, Jeffrey had arranged something special for them, and once again, Kelsey was curious as to what it would be. Tyler had sworn that it was less extravagant than their dinner in Florence had been, and Kelsey took him at his word. However, the dress she was wearing this evening gave her pause.

The black satin dress was stunning, and incredibly sexy. The front had detailed cutouts, and a slim band was the only thing that would cover her breasts. There was no bra that could work with this dress. The dress flared gently over her hips, and once the fabric had just reached the middle of her thighs, the fabric fell into a series of slits, connected only by thin, see-through mesh. Although nothing could be seen, little was left to the imagination. A high pair of black satin sandals completed the outfit. There was no purse to be seen, and Kelsey wondered if Jeffrey had forgotten to pack one. It didn't matter, because in their travels, Kelsey had bought two elegant clutch bags that were perfect for evenings out. She could take one of them tonight.

She stepped out of the bathroom carefully. The heels were very high, and it was clear to Kelsey that Jeffrey did not expect Kelsey to walk far in them. They showed off her bright red toenails beautifully.

"You picked this out, didn't you?" Kelsey asked Tyler. The last time she had worn a dress so revealing, Tyler had ordered it for her.

Tyler grinned. "I merely gave Jeffrey some direction," he replied. "You look gorgeous."

"Thank you," Kelsey replied. She felt gorgeous, although she could barely walk. She knew that Tyler would make allowances for her, wherever they were going. He wasn't a fan of high heels.

"Are you ready to go?"

"I just need to get my bag," Kelsey said.

"You don't need a bag," Tyler replied.

Kelsey looked at Tyler curiously. He held out his arm for her, and she took it.

"Trust me," he said.

"OK," Kelsey replied. And she did.

Kelsey laughed in delight a few moments later. They were on the upper level of the terrace of their suite, surrounded by sparkling lights and candles. Tyler pulled out Kelsey's chair at their elegant table for two, while their server and private chef worked on the second level of the terrace below them.

"This is amazing," Kelsey said.

"You said that you wanted to have dinner at home," Tyler said. "And I don't cook."

Kelsey giggled. "You do too," she said. "But this is really nice. Thanks, Tyler." She removed her shoes under the table and felt the cool tiles under her feet. Venice was a little warmer than Florence, and Kelsey's cashmere wrap was only a few steps away if she got cold.

Tyler reached out for Kelsey's hands across the table, and she took his. She felt the warm metal of his gold wedding band against her skin, and it made her smile.

"Is there anything special that you want to do tomorrow?" Tyler asked her. It would be their last full day in Venice. On Sunday, they would head back to Rome for the final five days of their vacation.

Kelsey shook her head. "No. Do you?"

"I want to buy Lisa some glass work," Tyler replied.

"Interesting," Kelsey said. "Why?" She peered at him. "Did you break something in her house?"

"When I was a kid. It wasn't important, but I'd like to try to replace it," Tyler replied.

"That's really sweet," Kelsey said.

Tyler shrugged. "I'm not sure how nice it is. I'm paying for it with her money."

Kelsey laughed. Although Lisa Olsen never made a big deal out of it, Tyler's billions all came from her hard work.

"It's the thought that counts," Kelsey replied.

Dinner was wonderful. Their chef had used the fresh-caught seafood that Venice was famous for, and had cooked it in traditional Italian styles. There were a half-dozen courses, each one more delectable than the next, and more than once Kelsey considered stealing food off Tyler's plate. She mostly managed to resist.

"More?" Tyler asked Kelsey, offering her another spoonful of berry tiramisu. She ate it off his spoon greedily. Their chef and server had left, taking everything but the three desserts with them.

"It's so good," Kelsey said.

"Margaret can make it for you," Tyler said. "Or Ryan."

Kelsey shook her head. "I'm so spoiled," she commented before opening her mouth for another spoonful of tiramisu. Tyler obliged her with another helping.

"Good. You should be," Tyler replied. He looked at her, put his hand behind her neck and gently pulled her forward for a kiss.

"More," Kelsey said.

Tyler kissed her again. "Or did you mean tiramisu?" he asked, offering her another spoonful.

"Both," Kelsey replied, licking raspberry jam from her lips.

Tyler surveyed her.

"Hurry up," he said. "We have business to attend to."

Kelsey giggled. "Now who's demanding?" she teased.

"Fine. Take your time," Tyler said. He took a spoonful of the berry tiramisu, and ate it very slowly and seductively off the spoon. Kelsey's eyes didn't leave his mouth, and she bit her own lip. She leaned toward him, and gave him a passionate kiss.

"Oh, now you're interested in me, now that I'm not feeding you tiramisu," Tyler said. He took another spoonful.

Kelsey surveyed him, then leaned close to him again.

"Share," she whispered.

"I think not," Tyler said. "You're not sharing with me. And," he noted, "there's only one spoon."

With a swift movement, Kelsey lifted some of the whipped cream off the side of the bowl with her finger, and ate it.

"I don't need a spoon," she replied sassily.

Tyler placed the spoon in his hand down on a cloth napkin.

"Share," he said to Kelsey. She placed her finger back in the bowl, and offered the whipped cream on it to Tyler. He licked it off her finger, and Kelsey felt electricity run down her spine.

"More," Tyler said.

"That's all you get," she cooed. She was lying.

"I don't think so," Tyler replied. "I think I can have it all." He ran his thumb around the edge of the tiramisu bowl and ate the whipped cream that collected on it. Kelsey watched every second, and bit her lip again.

"And I think you want to give it to me," Tyler added.

"No," Kelsey lied. "I'm not sharing."

"Fine," Tyler said. He stood up and picked up the glass tiramisu bowl.

"Hey, where are you going?" Kelsey asked.

"I'm going to eat my tiramisu," Tyler said with a shrug.

"Oh, you're going to be like that, are you?"

"I'm willing to share. You aren't," Tyler pointed out. "So I'm going to take it all. If you want some, come get it."

Kelsey felt warm and her breathing was fast. Tyler was still teasing her, but she wasn't sure if she wanted to be teased anymore. She wanted something else.

"I'll share with you, Tyler," she called out as he turned from her.

He turned back slowly. "You will?" he asked.

Kelsey nodded.

"Then take off your dress," Tyler replied.

Kelsey couldn't believe what she and Tyler had done, but there they were, lying under one of the enclosed areas of the terrace, and covered in what was left of the tiramisu. Tyler gently pulled something out of Kelsey's hair.

"Raspberry." he said, eating it.

"Tyler, how are we going to clean up?" Kelsey asked. It was a question that hadn't crossed her mind an hour earlier, when Tyler was licking whipped cream out of her belly button.

"I'm sure there's a hose," Tyler said unconcernedly.

"There was a point, when I first met you, when I thought I was the crazy one," Kelsey commented.

Tyler laughed. "You're here with me now," Tyler replied.

"Have you always lived your life like this?" Kelsey asked him.

"No, but you have," he replied. Kelsey stuck her tongue out at him and Tyler laughed again. She snuggled against him.

"At least it's warm," Kelsey said, as Tyler stroked her hair.

"It's a beautiful night. With my beautiful woman."

"You make me feel beautiful," Kelsey said. "Tonight was very special, and not just dessert. Thank you for arranging it for me."

"Anything for my princess," Tyler replied.

"That's true, isn't it?" Kelsey said. "You'll do anything for me."

"Pretty much," Tyler replied. "I'm not giving back my two billion dollars, though," he added.

Kelsey giggled. "I wouldn't ask you to. You'll need it to pay for this trip."

It was Tyler's turn to laugh. "It didn't cost that much, Kelsey," he replied.

"It feels like it did," Kelsey replied wistfully.

"Is something wrong?" Tyler asked suddenly.

There was, but Kelsey wasn't sure how to articulate it. So she just started to speak.

"I just feel so lucky to have you in my life," Kelsey said, and she felt tears come to her eyes when she said it. "I never thought I would be so happy, or feel so loved."

Tyler beamed and gave her a hug. He wiped a tear out of her eye.

"I think there's some jam there," he teased, and Kelsey laughed.

"I love you so much, Tyler," she said, wiping a tear away.

"I love you too, Princess," Tyler replied, holding her close.

Kelsey looked out at the night sky as she lay in Tyler's arms. The gentle wind blew over them, as they lay together, in love.

The next day Tyler and Kelsey went glass shopping for Lisa. Tyler ordered a dozen exquisite pieces, including vases and a small colorful chandelier, and arranged for them to be delivered to Seattle. That evening, they brought home a pizza and spent another night loving each other under the stars.

On Sunday, Kelsey sat in the private pool with Tyler, the remains of their breakfast a few feet away on a table.

"Looking forward to Rome?" Tyler asked her.

"Yeah, but it's going to be hard leaving here," Kelsey admitted. "At least I get to bring you along."

"You're stuck with me, beautiful," Tyler replied.

Kelsey stroked his face.

"There's no one else I'd rather be stuck with," she replied.

A few hours later, Kelsey was standing in the middle of a luxurious apartment, just five blocks from their previous hotel in Rome. Her arms were crossed and she was frowning at her husband.

"What do you mean I can pick which suite I want to stay in?" she asked.

"I rented the entire building," Tyler replied. "There are two suites. This one, and the one upstairs, which has a beautiful garden. Pick one."

Kelsey opened her mouth and closed it. Once again, she was at a loss for words.

"Kelsey," Tyler explained, "I don't really want the paparazzi finding us again. You can only imagine what will happen if they find out we're back in Rome."

Kelsey sighed. She could imagine. Another visit to the mayor would likely be in their future if they were caught.

"This way, we can come and go as we please. No one knows we're here, and there's no one to spot us."

"The concierge knows."

"She won't tell."

Kelsey let out a deep sigh and looked around the elegant room. It was historic — the apartment had once been the residence of Emperor Napoleon III. Classical art graced the walls, and fine antiques were everywhere.

"This is fine," Kelsey said in defeat.

"You haven't seen the garden suite," Tyler replied.

Kelsey sighed again, and Tyler smiled at her.

"Tell you what. We'll stay here tonight, move to the garden suite tomorrow, and you can decide which you prefer. OK?"

"OK. Thank you, Tyler."

"You're welcome, Kelsey," Tyler replied.

As they strolled down the Via dei Condotti to pick up one of Jessica's last-minute requests, Tyler had a question for Kelsey.

"Were you always this difficult?"

"Since you met me?"

"Since you were born."

Kelsey thought for a moment. "My mother says so," she replied.

"I'm not sure Kelly is the best judge. What does Dan say?"

"Dad's too biased. I'm his little girl. Anyway, he married my mom, and you know how difficult she is."

"True," Tyler agreed. "How about Grandma Rose? What would she say?"

Kelsey giggled. "That I've always been a handful," she replied.

"I thought so," Tyler said.

"You have a reputation yourself, Mr. Olsen, so don't judge me," Kelsey replied.

"I only drive Lisa crazy," Tyler said.

"I'm starting to understand why," Kelsey mused.

On Monday, Kelsey arrived back at the apartment after her morning run at the gym to a surprise.

Kelsey looked at Tyler, who looked back innocently.

"I thought Conor said no scooters," she commented.

Tyler shrugged. "There's no one to tell him," he replied with a smile.

Tyler drove with Kelsey on the back of the light blue Vespa, expertly weaving through Rome's traffic. Kelsey was exhilarated, and she knew that at least part of the reason was the thrill of breaking the rules. Tyler drove them into a beautiful park and he parked the scooter.

"Where are we?" Kelsey asked Tyler as he took her hand and led her onto a path.

"Villa Borghese. It's right behind our first hotel," Tyler replied.

"It's beautiful," Kelsey said, looking around at all of the green trees. Tyler said nothing, but just smiled.

After a few minutes of walking, Kelsey spotted a young man standing alone. A few yards away, a picnic was spread out on the lawn behind him. Kelsey supposed that he had been left behind by his picnic companions. Tyler steered Kelsey toward him.

"Are we lost?" she asked curiously.

"Not for long," Tyler replied. "*Ciao,*" he called out to the young man, who looked up from his phone.

Kelsey stood silently, holding Tyler's hand as Tyler and the young man had an animated conversation in Italian. At the end, the young man smiled at Kelsey and shook Tyler's hand.

"*Salve!*" he said as he walked off.

Kelsey turned and watched him leave. Then she looked at Tyler.

"Did I miss something?" she said.

"Give it a minute," Tyler replied confidently. Kelsey looked Tyler, then back at the young man. Finally, her eyes looked at the picnic.

"Now I understand," she said.

"Let's eat," Tyler said, walking her over to their picnic.

The picnic was beautifully laid out. In addition to the soft yellow picnic blanket, there were sunny yellow cushions and a wicker hamper. Tyler and Kelsey kicked off their shoes and arranged themselves on the blanket. Kelsey sat on a cushion next to the hamper, while Tyler lay his head on her lap.

"You're unbelievable, you know that, right?" Kelsey said. She reached into the hamper and pulled out a glass container full of strawberries.

"I'm glad you think so, Princess," Tyler replied.

They ate simple Italian food in the warm September sun. In addition to the food, there were flowers for Kelsey, and a bottle of sparkling lemonade.

"How do you have time to think of things like this?" Kelsey asked, removing the top of a strawberry for him. She offered the strawberry to him and Tyler took a bite.

He chewed, then said, "In all of the boring meetings I have to attend."

Kelsey laughed. "Not really," she said.

"No, it's completely true. I spend a lot of time thinking about you."

"I'm honored," Kelsey said, stroking his chestnut-brown hair with her hand.

Tyler looked up at her from his place in her lap.

"You actually listen to what's going on in your boring meetings, don't you?" he asked.

"If I don't, I don't know what's going on," Kelsey replied.

"Nothing's going on. The point of meetings is to pretend that something is," Tyler said.

"So cynical," Kelsey scolded, but she leaned down and kissed him.

"One more week," Tyler said thoughtfully, "Then I'll be sitting and pretending to listen again."

"What will you think about then?"

"Thanksgiving, I guess."

"Not the weekend?" Kelsey said.

"I try not to think about my weekends with you," Tyler said meaningfully. Kelsey looked at him curiously. "Because of what we usually spend our weekends doing," he explained.

"Visiting the babies?" Kelsey asked, confused.

Tyler laughed. "At night, Kels."

Kelsey blushed scarlet. "Of course. Right," she replied.

"My thoughts about you need to be G-rated," Tyler continued. "So I think of things we can do together."

"So what are you thinking about Thanksgiving? About staying in Seattle?" she asked hopefully.

"You know we can't," Tyler replied.

"I know," Kelsey replied. Her parents were expecting them.

"I've got to deliver you back to Dan safe and sound, otherwise I'm in trouble. Make sure you tell him you're having fun being married to me."

"I wonder what would happen if I didn't," Kelsey mused.

"No jokes, Mrs. Olsen."

"I wouldn't," Kelsey said, leaning down and giving Tyler another kiss. "I'm going to tell him you're the best husband ever."

"Thank you," Tyler said.

"And you'll do the same for me when we visit Lisa at Christmas. You'll tell her that I'm the perfect wife."

"Lisa won't care," Tyler said.

"You said that Lisa didn't care who you dated, and you were certainly wrong about that," Kelsey pointed out.

"We're married now. It's no longer an issue," Tyler said, with finality.

"Are you sure?" Kelsey said.

"What do you mean?" Tyler asked. He sat up. "Are you worried about Lisa?"

"I always worry about Lisa," Kelsey admitted.

Tyler lay back in Kelsey's lap. "Don't. She's fine," Tyler replied.

"That's why you just spent thousands of dollars on jewelry that I can take with me under the pre-nup," Kelsey said.

Tyler sat back up. "What do you want me to say?" he asked her.

"I want you to be honest with me."

"I am honest with you," Tyler replied.

"About Lisa?"

"About everything," Tyler replied.

"Then why are you saying that there isn't a problem, but acting like there is one?" Kelsey asked.

Tyler looked thoughtful. "I guess you have a point. That's what it must look like to you."

"What is it supposed to look like?" Kelsey asked.

Tyler sighed. "I don't know."

"What do you mean?" Kelsey asked.

"I don't know, Kelsey. I'm being honest with you. I believe that Lisa is going to leave you alone now, but I also think that I need to make sure that you're in the best financial position I can, while being mindful that there are a half-dozen people looking at my accounts to make sure that I don't actually transfer money to you."

"Why?" Kelsey demanded.

Tyler shook his head. "Just a feeling," he said.

"A feeling of what?" Kelsey pressed.

"Kelsey, I was blindsided by Lisa. I told you, I don't intend for it to happen again. I just want to have more control over what happens to us."

"Tyler, no one has total control over what happens to them. That's the reality of life. What's going on?"

Tyler sighed. "I've felt anxious a lot lately, and I'm starting to think that it's because I've been able to spend so much time with you. When I do, I can't help but think about how important you are to me, and how awful it was when you weren't with me."

"That's behind us," Kelsey said firmly. "We're together now."

"I know, but I can't shake the feeling that something's wrong. And until I figure out what it is, you're just going to have to get a bigger jewelry box."

Kelsey giggled. "You're so silly." she said, kissing him on the nose.

"Is that attractive to you?" Tyler asked.

"Everything about you is attractive to me," Kelsey replied.

"Good," Tyler said, lying back down in her lap.

Kelsey resumed running her fingers through his hair. "Ryan says you should meditate," Kelsey teased. "Get rid of that anxiety."

"Don't listen to Ryan," Tyler said. "He's insane."

"Have you heard from him since he forced Ellie on us?"

"Not a word. But remember, I'm ignoring my phone."

"Tyler," Kelsey scolded.

"We have one more week of vacation," Tyler replied. "And I'm going to make it count."

Kelsey was hot, sweaty, and totally exhausted as she looked at her husband hours later. He kissed her neck, and she clung to him, unable to speak. Her heart was pounding, and she could barely catch her breath. As Tyler kissed her again and again, Kelsey knew that there was no where else she would rather be.

"Hey, beautiful." Tyler said as Kelsey was gathering her things to go out on Tuesday morning.

"Yes?"

"Give me your phone," Tyler replied. Puzzled, Kelsey handed Tyler her Tactec phone.

"Thanks," Tyler said, placing it on the coffee table next to his own. "Are you ready?" he asked her, standing up from the sofa.

Kelsey pointed. "I need my phone."

"No, you don't. Not while we're in Rome."

"What do you mean?"

"We're taking a break from our phones on this visit. I don't want to get trapped into working again. We should have left them behind yesterday."

"Tyler, suppose someone needs us?" Kelsey asked.

"Who? We're in Rome." He looked at Kelsey. "Look, you can check it tonight to see if Jess wants you to buy anything else. It's after midnight in Seattle now anyway."

"Tyler, someone could want something important."

"No one ever calls us with anything important. If it's not Lorenzo setting us up again, it will be Lisa with some brilliant idea about how to improve shareholder value. It will wait."

"Tyler," Kelsey scolded.

"Kelsey, I just want to have fun with you while we're here this time," Tyler said. "Fun, without interruptions."

"How will I take pictures?"

"I'll bring my tablet and turn off internet access," Tyler said brightly.

Kelsey sighed in defeat. It would be strange not having her phone, but like Tyler, she wanted to enjoy their final few days in Rome.

"OK," she replied. "I'll leave it behind."

"Great," Tyler said, taking Kelsey's hand.

"So where are we going today?" Kelsey asked as Tyler led her down the stairs and out onto the street. They had stayed in the beautiful Garden Suite the previous night, and eaten breakfast on the lavender-plant-covered terrace.

"I need to buy you a present."

"You already bought me a present in Rome," Kelsey pointed out.

"I need to buy you another one. I couldn't find a jewelry store in Venice I wanted to take you to, so we'll buy another piece here."

"Tyler, I don't need any more jewelry."

"Of course you do. Becks wants us to dive right into the charity scene the second we get back," Tyler replied.

Kelsey knew from talking briefly with Becks that Seattle's social calendar was quite packed from late September through early November. As the new Mrs. Tyler Olsen, it meant that Kelsey would be wearing many beautiful dresses, and of course, the jewelry to match. Escorting Tyler would mean some balancing of time, but one thing that would probably work in Kelsey's favor is that Lisa Olsen would need an escort as well, so Bill Simon wouldn't be at work to complain that Kelsey wasn't there.

"Can I get something small?" Kelsey asked as they walked down the street.

"No," Tyler replied. "You got something small in Florence."

"The earrings have three carats of diamonds," Kelsey replied.

"They're tiny," Tyler said, and Kelsey wasn't sure that he was kidding.

"You're ridiculous," Kelsey commented.

Tyler kissed her hand. "That comment just added five thousand dollars to the cost of whatever we're buying today," he said.

"Tyler," Kelsey protested.

"Think of it this way, Kels. I'm not buying the jewelry for you. I'm buying it for Mrs. Tyler Olsen."

"That's me."

"You know what I mean. The Mrs. Tyler Olsen who has got to go to these events, and look expensive and make her husband, the future CEO of Tactec, look good. She can't just wear anything."

Kelsey sighed. Tyler had a point, although she didn't want to admit it. When she went out with Tyler, she would be an additional representative of the Olsen family's brand, much like Ellie was for the Librizzi family. At least Kelsey didn't have the limitations that Ellie had.

"So today we're buying jewelry for my persona?" Kelsey said.

"If you like," Tyler said, amused. "We can do other things too. Is there anything that we missed the last time we were here that you want to see?"

Kelsey shook her head.

"I just want to see you," she said. Tyler looked at her lovingly, and gave her a kiss.

Kelsey and Tyler spent the day away from their apartment, soaking up Rome. Since they had done so many tourist things on their first visit, this time they just strolled through the streets, stopped when they came across an interesting museum or statue, and enjoyed each other's company.

After buying a stunning diamond necklace for Mrs. Tyler Olsen and arranging for it to be shipped back to Seattle, they walked some more, always holding hands, always in love.

"You have your own gelato," Kelsey teased Tyler. They had eaten a late dinner near the Trevi fountain, and returned to the fountain to throw coins once again. On their way back to their apartment, they had stopped at a gelato place, and were in the process of eating it.

"Yours is tastier," Tyler replied.

"I told you that you should get hazelnut," Kelsey said.

"I didn't need to. You got hazelnut, and now you're sharing," Tyler replied, taking a bite of her cone.

Kelsey laughed delightedly. "Again with the sharing," she teased.

"I'll share with you, Princess," Tyler said seductively. "Any time."

Kelsey felt herself blush in the dark. She certainly liked what Tyler shared with her.

Tyler kissed her cheek and took another nibble of her cone.

There was a black town car sitting outside of their apartment building when they arrived on their street. As they approached, a man got out. It was Jeffrey.

"I thought I wasn't going to see you during my vacation," Tyler said to him irritably as they stopped next to the car.

Kelsey couldn't see Jeffrey's reaction in the dim streetlight.

"Lisa's trying to get in touch with you," Jeffrey replied.

"I'll talk to her tomorrow."

"She needs to talk to you now," Jeffrey said simply.

"Right now?" Tyler asked doubtfully.

"Yes," Jeffrey replied. He pulled out his phone and pressed a few buttons. He handed the phone to Tyler.

"I swear, if this isn't important, I'm firing you," Tyler said. He gave Kelsey a kiss. "One minute," he said to her. He walked a few steps away from the car.

Kelsey was holding a bag of Italian cookies that she and Tyler had bought during the day and was about to offer Jeffrey one, when Jeffrey said her name.

"Kelsey," Something in Jeffrey's voice gave Kelsey chills and she looked at him. Tyler was leaning against the wall of the building, Jeffrey's phone against his ear.

"Lisa is telling Tyler that his father was in a car accident in New York this morning," Jeffrey said quietly. He paused, then said, "They aren't sure Chris is going to survive."

Want my unreleased 5000-word story
Introducing the Billionaire Boys Club
and other free gifts from time to time?

Then join my mailing list at

http://www.caramillerbooks.com/inner-circle/

Subscribe now and read it now!

You can also follow me on Twitter and Facebook

Made in the USA
Middletown, DE
17 October 2023

40962952R00139